"How long are we gonna have to wait?" Nick whispered.

He heard her breath catch in her throat, saw her eyelashes flutter down. "As long as it takes."

Nick had no idea what she meant. As far as he was concerned, making love to Brittany had always felt right. He knew she wanted him. She'd always wanted him. It was there in her eyes.

"As long as what takes?" he asked.

Brittany felt a smile coming on. And then, everything inside her went perfectly still. Her thoughts, her breathing, even her heart seemed to stop for one brief moment. She wasn't certain that staying out of Nick's bed was luring him any closer to love, but she was falling a little farther, a little harder, every day.

Dear Reader,

This month, Romance is chock-full of excitement. First, VIRGIN BRIDES continues with *The Bride's Second Thought,* an emotionally compelling story by bestselling author Elizabeth August. When a virginal bride-to-be finds her fiancé with another woman, she flees to the mountains for refuge…only to be stranded with a gorgeous stranger who gives her second thoughts about a lot of things….

Next, Natalie Patrick offers up a delightful BUNDLES OF JOY with *Boot Scootin' Secret Baby.* Bull rider Jacob "Cub" Goodacre returns to South Dakota for his rodeo hurrah, only to learn he's still a married man…and father to a two-year-old heart tugger. BACHELOR GULCH, Sandra Steffen's wonderful Western series, resumes with the story of an estranged couple who had wed for the sake of their child…but wonder if they can rekindle their love in *Nick's Long-Awaited Honeymoon.*

Rising star Kristin Morgan delivers a tender, sexy tale about a woman whose biological clock is booming and the best friend who consents to being her *Shotgun Groom.* If you want a humorous—red-hot!—read, try Vivian Leiber's *The 6'2", 200 lb. Challenge.* The battle of the sexes doesn't get any better! Finally, Lisa Kaye Laurel's fairy-tale series, ROYAL WEDDINGS, draws to a close with *The Irresistible Prince,* where the woman hired to find the royal a wife realizes *she* is the perfect candidate!

In May, VIRGIN BRIDES resumes with Annette Broadrick, and future months feature titles by Suzanne Carey and Judy Christenberry, among others. So keep coming back to Romance, where you're sure to find the classic tales you love, told in fresh, exciting ways.

Enjoy!

Joan Marlow Golan

Joan Marlow Golan
Senior Editor, Silhouette Romance

Please address questions and book requests to:
Silhouette Reader Service
U.S.: 3010 Walden Ave., P.O. Box 1325, Buffalo, NY 14269
Canadian: P.O. Box 609, Fort Erie, Ont. L2A 5X3

Sandra Steffen

NICK'S LONG-AWAITED HONEYMOON

Silhouette

ROMANCE™

Published by Silhouette Books

America's Publisher of Contemporary Romance

For my five "grown" nieces and nephew—
Karen, Kathie, Laurie, Jerry and Pattie. I married into this family, and you were born into it. Was it fate or luck? It's hard to say. I only know that you're all so easy to love, and I'm proud to be your aunt.

 SILHOUETTE BOOKS

ISBN 0-373-19290-8

NICK'S LONG-AWAITED HONEYMOON

SANDRA STEFFEN

Creating memorable characters is one of Sandra's favorite aspects of writing. She's always been a romantic and is thrilled to be able to spend her days doing what she loves—bringing her characters to life on her computer screen.

Sandra grew up in Michigan, the fourth of ten children, all of whom have taken the old adage "Go forth and multiply" quite literally. Add to this her husband, who is her real-life hero, their four school-age sons who keep their lives in constant motion, their gigantic cat, Percy, and her wonderful friends, in-laws and neighbors, and what do you get? Chaos, of course, but also a wonderful sense of belonging she wouldn't trade for the world.

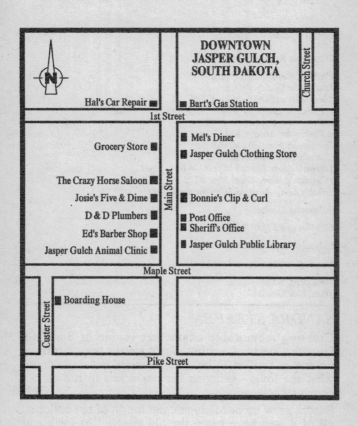

DOWNTOWN JASPER GULCH, SOUTH DAKOTA

Church Street

Hal's Car Repair ■   ■ Bart's Gas Station

1st Street

Grocery Store ■

■ Mel's Diner

■ Jasper Gulch Clothing Store

The Crazy Horse Saloon ■

Josie's Five & Dime ■

■ Bonnie's Clip & Curl

D & D Plumbers ■

■ Post Office

Ed's Barber Shop ■

■ Sheriff's Office

Jasper Gulch Animal Clinic ■

■ Jasper Gulch Public Library

Main Street

Maple Street

Custer Street

■ Boarding House

Pike Street

Chapter One

He wasn't lost. Nick Colter had a sixth sense about direction. It came in handy in back alleys and bad situations. No, he wasn't lost. Custer Street, on the other hand, was lost as hell. Street signs would have been nice. For some strange reason only half the streets in this town had them.

He inched his car to a corner and peered in every direction. Jasper Gulch, South Dakota, wasn't much different from fifty other towns he'd passed on his way from Chicago. The houses were at least a hundred years old and looked as if they'd seen better days. Porch lights were on, but the dwellings themselves were dark. Nick shook his head. Might as well hang a sign out front for burglars: "House empty. Take your time. The good silver is in the pantry."

"Careful, Colter," he muttered under his breath. "One of these days somebody's gonna accuse you of being cynical."

His next turn landed him back on Main Street where he'd started. He strummed his fingers on the steering wheel and studied his surroundings. The street was lined with cars and pickup trucks, but not a single person was in sight. Spotting a lit building a block over, he parked his car in the first available space and headed inside.

He gave the room a sweeping glance the instant he set foot inside the door. A wedding reception was taking place, and if the volume of the boot-stomping music coming from the country-western band and the laughter and raised voices of the crowd were an accurate indication, the folks of Jasper Gulch were having a good time. Only a few of the wedding guests noticed his presence—a handful of kids who stopped their game of tag to stare at him, two teenaged girls who whispered behind their hands, and an old man whose thumbs were hooked through his suspenders.

"Can I help you, son?" the old cowboy asked.

Keeping his eyes and ears open, Nick said, "I don't make a habit of crashing wedding receptions, but I can't seem to find Custer Street."

"You visiting," the other man asked, scratching his craggy chin, "or just passing through?"

"Visiting, I suppose."

The old man nodded. "Then you must be lookin' for the boardin' house. No sense goin' there right now. The owner's not home. I'm Cletus McCully. We ain't much for standing on ceremony around here, so you might as well grab yerself a cup of that there punch and join the party."

Nick tried to pass on the punch. Cletus would hear nothing of it. With a shake of his head and a snap of one suspender, the old man ambled away to get it himself. Nick put the minute of solitude to good use, systematically giving the town hall a more thorough once-over. White streamers trailed from the ceiling. A half-eaten wedding cake sat on a small table. The three-piece band was set up in one corner, a table piled high with gifts in another. Most of the men wore bolo ties and cowboy boots while the women wore calico dresses or Western skirts. So far he hadn't seen a man with a sinister leer, a silver ponytail and a jagged scar.

"What's going on, on the dance floor?" he asked as Cletus shoved a cup of punch into his hand.

"Follow me," Cletus muttered. "Maybe we can get a better view from the other side."

It wasn't difficult to keep up with the old man's bow-legged gait. Keeping up with his conversation was another matter. The man talked about people Nick couldn't possibly know, telling him about the weddings that had taken place since the boys had decided to put an ad in the papers luring women to *this-here* neck of the woods. In a very short amount of time Nick had learned that someone named DoraLee had eloped with a local rancher named Boomer, Cletus's grandson Wyatt had snagged one of the first gals to come to town, and his granddaughter, Melody, had married the "boy" she'd been in love with most of her life. Today's bride was a Southern belle named Pamela Sue, the groom a mama's boy named Grover.

"One by one the new gals who've moved to town are bitin' the bullet," Cletus declared. "I'm afraid none of the ones who're left are makin' it easy on the poor Jasper Gents. Crystal Galloway, the newest gal in town, is a looker, but she's got a mouth on her that could scare the average sailor clean away."

Other than nodding now and then when it was expected of him, Nick kept silent. Listening with only one ear, he made a sweeping perusal of every person in the room. The first glimpse of a shaggy, gray ponytail on the other side of the hall had the hairs on the back of his neck standing on end. Homing in on a silver-haired man in the shadows, everything inside Nick went perfectly still.

"Then there's our own Louetta Graham," Cletus was saying, "but I'm afraid she's so shy it's almost hopeless. That only leaves the girls fresh out of school and the new gal who bought the boarding house. She's a pretty little thing, that's for sure, but she's mighty stubborn, too."

Nick flexed his fingers at his sides, squinting into the shadows across the room. The man was the right height, but the cowboy hat was deceiving. Nick checked the exits, gauging the most direct route to cover, just in case things took an ugly turn.

"I tried my darnedest to get that gal to reach for the bouquet..."

Nick was barely listening now, all his attention trained on the length of shaggy hair across the room.

"But she says since her divorce ain't final, she ain't really single. Like I told her, if that husband of hers was dim-witted enough to let her get away, a few weeks one way or the other won't make any difference whatsoever. Says she don't feel married. Problem is, I don't think Brittany feels unmarried, either."

The silver-haired man stepped out of the shadows at the same instant Cletus uttered the one name in all the world that could bring Nick to his knees. He was caught between two force fields. Danger. And need. Blood pounded in his head, and his lungs felt too large for his chest.

The silver-haired man turned, giving Nick a good look at his face. The guy was sixty years old if he was a day and sported a handlebar mustache and a hefty paunch. His face was deeply lined, but there was no jagged scar. It wasn't his man.

It didn't take long for the roaring din in Nick's ears to quiet. The brick in his chest was going to be more difficult to eliminate.

"I'm hoping it's only a matter of time before one of our shy-but-willin' Jasper Gents catches Brittany's eye and sweeps her off her feet, but I'm afraid it might be more complicated than that. She says it's just semantics—whatever in tarnation that means—and has nothin' to do with the fact that her soon-to-be ex-husband is paying her a little visit in a couple of days."

The old man's voice trailed away. Peering up at Nick through bushy white eyebrows, he said, "I don't believe I caught your name, son."

The crowd parted, and Nick had his first clear view of a

slender, dark-haired woman who was trying to ward off the advances of one of the cowboys on the other side of the dance floor. The man brushed aside a lock of her chin-length hair and bent his head as if he wanted to whisper something in her ear. Instead, he planted a sloppy kiss on one corner of her mouth.

Nick's fingers curled around the cup in his hand. Handing it back to Cletus, he said, "My name's Nick Colter. That dim-witted husband you mentioned. You'll have to excuse me. There's a man I have to punch in the nose."

"Now don't be too hasty there…"

Nick moved with the same kind of purpose he used in the streets and alleys of Chicago, maneuvering around the people blocking his path so quickly they had to turn their heads to keep him in their line of vision. He stopped behind the cowboy and tapped him on the shoulder with enough force to leave no doubt that Nick meant business.

The man spun around so fast he teetered slightly. "What the—"

"Pardon me," Nick ground between clenched teeth, "but I don't appreciate watching another man kiss my wife."

"Your wife?"

Brittany Matthews's decision to step between the two men who were squaring off opposite each other wasn't made consciously. Once she'd done it she wasn't sure it had been wise. Now she had a half-drunken cowboy behind her and an angry man in front of her. She had no doubt which of the two was going to be more difficult to deal with.

"Nick."

His eyes were narrowed, accenting sculpted cheekbones and a slightly crooked nose. His hair was dark and just wavy enough to be unruly. His mouth was set in a straight line, his chin squared in a manner that had always meant trouble. There were taller men in the room. But none were more intimidating. Nick's striking blue eyes were his one feature that could be soft. Right now they were shooting daggers at the man behind her. "Step aside, Brittany. This won't take long."

Brittany heard the murmur going through the crowd. Swallowing, she was more aware of the murmur going through her. She'd spent the better part of the past week preparing herself to see Nick again. If he had arrived when he said he would, she might have been prepared. Or maybe nothing could prepare a woman for the sight of the man who had been her first lover, and her greatest heartache.

She studied him thoughtfully for a moment, trying to get her emotions under control. Finally she shook her head and said, "You don't have any reason to pick a fight with Forrest, Nick."

Nick's lip curled. "I think anytime a man's wife is caught kissing another man is cause for a fight."

"She told me she's gettin' a divorce," the other man slurred.

Groaning out loud, Brittany snagged Nick's hand and pulled him to a more-secluded spot on the floor. "I didn't kiss him, you idiot."

"You gonna give me a lesson on who puts what where?"

"Come on, Nick. Forrest is half-drunk."

"Did you like it?"

"Did I—" She bristled. Nick Colter made her so mad.

"Well?" he prodded.

Oh, for heaven's sakes. "Did it look like I liked it?"

"What the hell kind of answer is that?"

Brittany took a fortifying breath and willed herself to refrain from saying what she was thinking. Taking the utmost care to instill her voice with patience, she said, "What are you doing here tonight, Nick? I thought you said you weren't coming until Monday."

Nick ran a hand through his hair and glanced at the man with the silver ponytail and handlebar mustache. What *was* he doing here? There was a question. Turning his attention back to Brittany, he thought a better one would have been How did he ever let her go? Suddenly he felt very tired, and very alone.

Releasing a pent-up breath, he said, "I cleared up everything back home and took off a couple of days early. How are you, Brittany? And how's Savannah?"

There was nothing Brittany could do to keep her heart from sliding into her stomach. Angry, Nick Colter was a force to be reckoned with. Nice, he was almost impossible to resist. Fighting valiantly to do just that, she gave in to a heartfelt sigh. "I'm fine, Nick. And so is Savannah. She fell asleep a little while ago. She's going to be tickled to see you."

Leading the way to a table on the far side of the room, she felt the eyes of half the people in town, yet she was more aware of Nick's gaze following her every move. He'd always been able to undress her with his eyes. No matter what else had gone wrong between them, her husband had always been an earthy, virile man. *Her soon-to-be ex-husband,* she reminded herself. Training her eyes on her six-year-old daughter's dark head nestled in the hollow of Crystal Galloway's shoulder, Brittany hurried through the crowd.

"Well, well," Crystal exclaimed, watching them advance. "Who have we here?"

Hoping her friend would attribute this sudden attack of breathlessness on her brisk trek across the room, Brittany said, "Crystal, this is Nick Colter. Savannah's father."

"Nice to meet you," Nick said.

With delicate eyebrows arched knowingly, Crystal extended her right hand. Nick shook it, but strangely, his fingers didn't linger.

Crystal smiled. "Charmed I'm sure."

Brittany glanced up at Nick. She'd been wondering how he would react to Crystal. She wasn't jealous. It just so happened that she thought the world of her new friend. But Crystal was gorgeous. And men always noticed, which made them easy targets for her flirtations. Nick's attention had already shifted back to *her* as if seeing a buxom blonde with startling green eyes was no big deal. Brittany absolutely, positively forbade herself to melt.

"Taste this punch, Brittany," Crystal said, holding up a paper cup.

Thankful to have something to do with her hands, Brittany lifted the cup to her lips. Two hours ago the punch had been sweet. Now, it warmed a path from her throat to her stomach where it curled outward in waves.

She glanced around the room, suddenly understanding the reason why the noise level was bordering on a dull roar. The punch was spiked. From the depth and heartiness of the men's guffaws and the silliness of the women's laughter, it had been that way for some time.

"Can you believe Isabell missed it?" Crystal asked, pointing to a gray-haired woman who bore an amazing likeness to the cartoon character Olive Oyl, and was twittering louder than anybody else.

Brittany smiled at the spectacle Isabell Pruitt and Opal Graham, two of the staunchest leaders of the Jasper Gulch Ladies Aid Society, were making from the center of the dance floor. "It looks like they've made up," she said, thinking of all the months it had been since the former best friends had spoken. Cheeks flushed and chins bobbing, they moved their hands and shook their hips in a manner that looked very little like the dance they were trying to do.

"Isabell and Opal doing the Bunny Hop. Now there's one for your history books, Brittany," Crystal declared.

"Everybody's getting sloshed," Nick said, tossing the cup into a nearby trash can. "Reminds me of your senior prom. Somebody spiked the punch that night, too. Remember?"

Brittany didn't intend to meet his eyes. Once she had, she couldn't look away. He was gazing at her much as he had that night all those years ago. He'd been young and defiant then. He wasn't much different now. Neither of them had touched a drop of alcohol that night. Brittany had felt intoxicated without it, drunk on whimsy and on love.

Nick had rented a tux for the prom, when she knew darn well he couldn't afford it. Nick Colter had always been proud, had always been intent upon impressing her. What he'd never understood was that he didn't have to try to impress her. She'd been a girl on the brink of womanhood. He'd been the first boy to kiss her with his tongue, the first boy to touch her breasts, the first boy to make her heart speed up and her breathing deepen. She could practically hear the rasp her dress zipper had made as he'd lowered it after the prom. She could practically feel that first touch of his hand on her naked skin. She'd been so certain he'd loved her, and so filled with the vehemence of youth. They'd managed to keep from going all the way that night. But they'd both known it was only a matter of time.

She came back to the present slowly. Nick was breathing through his mouth, a muscle working in one cheek much the way it had when he'd walked her to her door that night all those years ago. She still sighed when she thought about how reluctant she'd been to allow the night to end.

Crystal cleared her throat, reminding Brittany that she and Nick weren't alone. "How old were you two when you met?" Crystal asked.

"Brittany was seventeen," Nick answered. "I was two years older."

"You went together for a long time, didn't you? You must have known each other pretty well."

Brittany didn't know how to answer. She'd thought she'd known him. As the years had gone by, she'd begun to realize that knowing someone wasn't always enough. Suddenly feeling as if she could use a stiff drink herself, she gave herself a mental shake and said, "I should take Savannah home."

She reached for their child, but Nick beat her there. It required little effort to lift Savannah into his arms. She was petite like her mother, but he pretended to stagger beneath her weight. "She's grown."

Brittany nodded. "She just turned six."

Nick knew how old his little girl was. He remembered every detail of the night she was born, just as he remembered every detail of the night she was conceived.

She stirred, smiling at him before her eyes had completely opened. "Daddy."

"Hi, Savannah-banana."

"Are you still mad at Mommy and me?" she asked.

Nick closed his eyes and shook his head. "I was angry, Savannah, but never at you or Mommy."

He was almost glad when Brittany didn't meet his gaze, not that she was fooling him with the way she pretended that all her attention was trained on getting Savannah into a small red coat. She was aware of the strong emotions between them, and so was he.

A helluva lot more people noticed Nick's exit than had noticed his entry into the room. He could practically hear the speculation behind their stares. After all, he was leaving with a beautiful woman who happened to be his wife.

"Where's your car?" he asked from the top step.

Brittany went down to the sidewalk before answering. "I came with Crystal."

It was the end of March, and officially spring. A person couldn't prove it by the snow clinging to the ground or the wind cutting through his clothing. Anxious to get Savannah and Brittany inside where it was safe and warm, Nick said, "Come on, my car's over here."

He made short work of the drive to Custer Street, thanks to Brittany's simple directions. Her house was located in the middle of the block on one of the streets that didn't have a sign. He'd driven past it earlier, just as he'd driven past every other house in town. While Brittany helped Savannah from the car, Nick reached into the back seat for his duffel bag and a battered old suitcase. With a case in each hand, he took a moment to study his surroundings. The house looked as old as all the other houses in town, but this one was larger than most and had a high roof, a long front porch and burgundy siding that set it apart from the others.

Brittany took a key from her purse and unlocked the front door. Eyeing the mechanism, Nick wondered why she bothered. The lock was old and could have been jimmied with a screw driver, a credit card, or a bent paper clip, for that matter.

"Mommy said you weren't coming until Monday," Savannah said, still holding her mother's hand.

Nick's gaze swept his daughter's face. He knew before she batted her eyelashes that he was a goner. He could interrogate hardened criminals, yet one innocent statement from that little scrap of a girl had him scrambling for an explanation. He *had* planned to arrive on Monday. But he hadn't planned on this driving need to get here sooner. Saying the only thing he could think of that was still the truth, he said, "I've missed you."

"Are you going to stay, Daddy?"

He glanced up and found Brittany watching him. "For a while," he said quietly, and left it at that.

All three of them walked inside, Brittany turning lights on as she went. "It's past your bedtime, Savannah. Tell Daddy good-night."

"But Daddy just got here."

Nick almost smiled at the shrillness in Savannah's voice. It was definitely an improvement on the nightmares followed by long stretches of silence she'd been having a year ago. Going down on his haunches, he said, "Mommy's right. We're all tired tonight. Tomorrow, when we're rested, we'll spend the whole day together."

"Promise?"

His throat convulsed and all but closed. How many promises had he failed to keep these past seven years? "I promise, Savannah."

Her smile finished the job to his throat, her arms winding shyly around his neck. "Good night, Daddy."

He must have answered, because Savannah allowed her mother to lead her from the room without a struggle. Nick hovered in the doorway until they were out of sight. Then, testing the shakiness of his legs, he strode into the next room and the next. There was an old-fashioned kitchen with a monstrous antique stove and a round oak table, a bathroom with a claw-footed tub and green tile floor. A door led to the backyard via a laundry room. Another door led to the side yard off the kitchen. In fact, as far as he could tell, there were three exterior doors on the main floor. And enough low windows with faulty, or no, locks to make him shudder. The house had all the security of a chicken coop.

The floor creaked slightly, alerting him to Brittany's presence behind him. "What are you doing, Nick?"

Trying for nonchalance, he crossed his arms and slowly turned around. "Is Savannah asleep?"

At her nod, he realized he'd been lost in thought longer than he'd realized. Shrugging, he said, "I guess I was snooping. This is quite a house."

"It has seven bedrooms," she answered. "That's a lot of rooms to heat, believe me."

Nick thought they were a lot of rooms for someone to hide in.

"Isn't it incredible?" she asked, spreading her arms wide to encompass the entire house.

The light was on in the kitchen behind him and in the living room behind her, but not in the tiny alcove where they were both standing. As if she didn't think it was wise to stay too long in a darkened room with him, she took a backward step, then deftly led the way through another door.

Nick followed as far as the doorway. Leaning one hip against the oak trim, he watched her switch on a low lamp.

"At one time this was used as a study," she said. "It's my favorite room. This house was one of the first to be built in Jasper Gulch and belonged to the first doctor to settle in this part of the territory."

She strode to a low table where she turned on another lamp. The soft bulb cast shadows into the corners, delineating the curve of her hip through the thin fabric of her dress. She was talking about the history of the house, but Nick couldn't stop thinking about the history between them. He took a step toward her, propelled by the need to be closer and something else he'd never fully understood.

Her hair looked even darker in the soft lamplight. Tendrils curled over the collar of her green dress and clung to her cheeks, accenting the delicate hollows below her cheekbones and the darkness of her eyes. She slanted him a look, then immediately started to speak, as if she thought talking would break the pull that had always been between them. He could have told her there was nothing she could do to accomplish that, but he didn't want her to stop talking. Lord, he'd missed the clear, sultry sound of her voice.

"See those books?" she asked, gesturing to a tall bookcase. "Some of them are the very texts Doctor Avery used to treat patients. I think he used this room as an examination room when he first started his practice." She moved again, this time to sweep a thick curtain aside. "Look at this. Fur traders and Indians and later gold seekers and cowboys could come right in without traipsing through the rest of the house."

Nick stared at the narrow oak panels behind the curtain. *Make that four doors leading directly to the outside.*

"Nick, what is it?"

Nick heard the hesitation in her voice, saw it in her eyes. He didn't know what to tell her, how much to tell her, if he should tell her at all. He waited a moment too long to come up with an answer, because she straightened, bristling.

"I was hoping you would try to keep an open mind."

Ignoring the stiffness he'd acquired during his twelve-hour drive from Chicago, he tried to decide whether to be relieved or angry that she'd automatically jumped to the wrong conclusion. "Don't I always keep an open mind?"

"Pu-lease."

"What?"

She was staring at him, mouth gaping. "Since when have you been open-minded about anything?"

He started to speak, closed his mouth and tried again, only to repeat the process. By the time he'd thought of an answer, she was trying not to smile. He almost couldn't speak all over again. "Well," he finally said, "I didn't punch Forrest in the nose when he kissed you tonight."

"It was very big of you to refrain from hitting a man who was making an innocent pass at me in a crowded room, Nick."

He stared at her silently, then took a step closer.

"What?" she asked.

"Oh. I was just thinking about the first time I saw you. It seems to me you were with another man that night, too."

Brittany took careful note of Nick's features and calmly crossed her arms. "I was *not* with another man tonight. And the night we met I was with a boy."

"Your hair was long then," he said as if she hadn't spoken. "It hung straight and shimmery halfway down your back. Every time I looked at it I knew I had to wrap my hands in it. Never mind that you were too young, too innocent and way too good for a boy like me."

Brittany knew she should put a stop to all this reminiscing. Just as she knew she had to put the past in perspective. And she would, as soon as she got her bearings and reminded herself of her resolve. That had always been hard to do with Nick. If he had walked directly to her, she could have put her hand up to ward off his advance. But he only took one slow, easy step at a time, and he kept talking in that same easy way he had, melting her resolve one degree at a time.

"Never mind that I had a bear of an exam to take at the police academy at 8:00 a.m. the next morning and my brother would have had my butt in a sling if I was late," he said, his blue eyes now as soft and mellow as lamplight.

Brittany tried to swallow the hoarseness in her throat. "We went out for burgers, Nick, and talked until midnight. But you never touched my hair that night."

"I was imagining it the whole time, savoring the moment, enjoying the anticipation." He reached up and threaded his fingers through the hair at her ear.

"It isn't long anymore," she whispered.

He closed his eyes. And she knew he was savoring again. A muscle convulsed in his throat and his lips parted. And then, as if he'd had all the savoring he could stand, he pulled her to him and covered her mouth with his.

His kiss was as familiar as the sound of her own name, his scent one that could never be bottled. She breathed it all the way to the bottom of her lungs, the scent of man and soap and cold winter air. Her own eyes drifted closed, her lips parting beneath his.

His mouth moved over hers like a man a long time denied. He'd always kissed her like this, even the first time. He'd swept her off her feet that night. And she'd let him. She didn't blame him. And she didn't blame herself. She'd been a lonely girl in another new town, and he'd been a dark, brooding nineteen-year-old with a bad-boy smile and an amazingly kind heart. She'd been hopelessly in love with him. Also hopelessly naive. She'd latched on to him for stability, when she should have been nurturing her own fledgling strength.

She was older now and wiser and, God help her, stronger. Strong enough to put an end to what was happening between them before it burned out of control.

He groaned what sounded like her name. Deepening the kiss, he wrapped his arms around her back, molding her to every hard inch of him. Even as she sighed his name she knew what she had to do. She shuddered, turning her face an inch and then two. Sucking in a ragged breath of air, she straightened her spine and let her arms fall away from his waist.

He kissed her cheek, her temple, the delicate ridge of her ear, moaning in protest when she shook her head.

"Nick. We can't do this. Not anymore."

Chapter Two

"Please, Nick. We have to stop."

Nick heard Brittany's hoarse whisper. He felt her stiffen, her arms going limp at her sides. His breathing was ragged, his body so taut with need he couldn't see straight.

Stop?

He never wanted to stop. But Brittany was drawing away, pulling out of his embrace. And he had no choice but to let her go. Just as he'd had no choice six months ago when she'd told him she wanted to move to Jasper Gulch, South Dakota.

"That shouldn't have happened, Nick."

He could have argued. Heaven knew he was good at it. But the dull and troubled edge in her voice kept him silent.

"I don't know *how* it happened," she said quietly.

There was no controlling the sound he made deep in his throat. He knew exactly how it had happened. The same way it had always happened between them. They could be talking one minute, arguing, even, and the next thing either of them knew they were tangled up in sheets.

Tonight Brittany hadn't let it get to that point. She was

standing across from him in the narrow room, glancing from him to her watch and back again. "It's late."

Too late? he wanted to ask.

Her eyes pleaded with him not to, so he took a deep breath and made a feeble stab at idle conversation, instead. They exhausted the topic of the weather in about ten seconds. After that they talked about Savannah. Brittany seemed relieved, and latched on to the subject, rattling off the name of Savannah's teacher and her new best friend. He'd spoken to Savannah on the telephone often, so he already knew her favorite subject was math, but he let Brittany tell him, anyway. Since they both loved their daughter to distraction, talking about her was safe. Or at least as safe as any subject was for them.

He followed Brittany into the kitchen where she brewed tea for herself. She didn't have any beer, but she offered him a soda. They took their drinks to the living room and sat in the comfortable old furniture, he on the sofa, she with her feet curled underneath her on a matching overstuffed chair, her high-heeled shoes sitting crookedly on the carpet below. They could have been two friends talking late on a Saturday night. Except they'd always been more than friends.

When they ran out of things to say about their daughter, Brittany told him about some of the history she'd learned about Jasper Gulch. Every now and then the wind rattled a windowpane or a shutter. Nick was aware of every sound, but little by little the smooth cadence of Brittany's voice worked over him. His soda grew warm as she spun tales of the man who'd founded this town and others who had come to help him. Few people had Brittany's gift for bringing the past to life, describing the people of another time as if she'd lived there with them. She would have made a marvelous teacher. No doubt every little boy in her class would have had a crush on her.

Her eyes were so dark he couldn't see the pupils from here, but there was no disguising the interest in their depths. "Jasper Carson arrived here from the Black Hills more than a hundred years ago with a widow he'd won in a poker game at his side and a little gold in his pocket," she explained. "He married the woman and founded the town, but it was Abigail Carson who gave the town its name."

Intrigued by the story, Nick settled himself more comfortably into the cushions, listening to her tale.

"Local legend paints Jasper as a rugged, handsome, exasperating man. If you ask any of the Carsons alive today they'll claim they've inherited each and every one of those traits. According to Jasper's journals, Abigail was none too happy with her fate. It seemed she wouldn't give her new husband the time of day, if you know what I mean."

Nick almost blurted out that only a woman could make such a statement so soon after being kissed so thoroughly, so completely by a man who knew every inch of her body, every nuance of her personality, the meaning behind every one of her sighs. Clearing his throat that had suddenly gone dry, he said, "Did she? Finally give him the time of day, I mean."

Brittany smiled, warming to the tale. "Evidently he won on that point, but lost on the one about the town's name. Abigail grew to love him, but she insisted they name the town after his first name, instead of his last. Thus, Jasper Gulch was born, followed in close succession by three Carson sons."

"Then their marriage was built on give and take and survived in the midst of incredible odds."

Her smile faded. "Nick."

He sat forward, elbows resting on his thighs, his hands folded as if in prayer. "I know what you're going to say, Brittany. I know we've been over this a thousand times. Believe me, I know. But I also know that what we shared in the doctor's study twenty minutes ago was pretty damned incredible. I can't just forget it. Can you?"

She jumped to her feet and paced to the other side of the room. "You're right. We have been over this a thousand times. We've said it all a thousand different ways, with caution and confusion, in anger, in defiance, in disbelief and in tears.

You and I both know the attraction has always been explosive between us. But we also know our problems have a way of returning with the dawn.''

She came to a stop near the kitchen, her vehemence fading to a kind of acceptance Nick liked a lot less. He didn't remember standing up, but as long as he was on his feet, he strode closer. As she watched him, her eyes grew round and wary. It hurt more than any insult she could have uttered, and stopped him in his tracks.

''I've missed you, you know.''

Her shoulders sagged. ''I know. I've missed you, too. And so has Savannah.''

Nick ran a hand through his hair. He wanted to shout in frustration. And then he wanted to carry Brittany to the nearest bed and make love to her all night long. He wanted them to give their marriage another chance. He already knew what she would say if he whispered his wish out loud: ''We've given our marriage another chance a hundred times.''

And they had.

The marriage counselor they'd seen had been quick to attribute their problems to their childhoods. Nick had already known who was to blame, and it wasn't his mother. He was twenty-nine years old, and he'd spent most of the ten years he'd known Brittany trying to make things right.

''We're hopeless, aren't we?'' she said quietly.

Nick shook his head. ''I'm hopeless. You're beautiful.''

He was vaguely aware of a sound in the foyer, but he couldn't seem to pull his gaze away from Brittany's sad smile. The door opened before he came to his senses.

''Yoo-hoo, we're home.''

Nick swung around and swore under his breath. He'd seen corpses with a better reaction time than his had been.

Home? he thought, recovering slightly. Exactly how many people lived here?

Crystal Galloway closed the door for a frail, little old lady. ''We would have been here sooner,'' she said, slipping an arm around the old lady's shoulders, "but Mertyl wanted to do the chicken dance one more time." Pointing to the back of Mertyl's head, Crystal mouthed, "She's sloshed."

"Mertyl," Brittany said, reacting to Crystal's head gesture, "you must be exhausted."

A cat meowed its way down the open stairway, landing in Mertyl's arms with a thud that nearly toppled her. The old lady mumbled something Nick couldn't make out. She listened for a moment before mumbling something else. He didn't know who was keeping up the other end of the conversation, but even her overweight yellow cat looked at her strangely.

Mertyl couldn't have weighed more than ninety-five pounds. Obviously she couldn't hold her liquor. Her eyes were a little too bright, her smile crooked, her head nodding like those toy dogs people put in the back windows of their cars. She was a head shorter than Crystal and was getting shorter by the second. Nick made it to her side and had her back on her feet before her knees gave out.

"Beautiful bride, just beautiful," Mertyl declared out of the blue. "Cake was a mite dry, but the punch was the best I ever tasted."

"Come on, dear," Crystal said from Mertyl's other side. "Let's get Daisy settled upstairs. Want me to show Nick to a room, too?" she asked Brittany.

Brittany felt Nick's eyes on her, but *her* gaze was trained on Crystal. There was something exotic about the shape of Crystal's green eyes and the way they peered out at the world beneath all that wavy blond hair. The two of them had become fast friends soon after Crystal had moved to Jasper Gulch three months ago. Soul sisters, Crystal called them. The woman could speak her mind one minute, bare her soul the next and put a person in his or her place without batting an eye. Right now, in her own straightforward way, she was offering Brittany a reprieve. That would allow Brittany to put a little distance between her and Nick, and she could put things back into perspective.

Feeling less shaky, Brittany looked at Nick. He stared back at her, a muscle working in one lean cheek. She'd missed him these past six months, but she hadn't missed the upheaval he brought back into her life. It wasn't anything he did. It was the way she felt when he was near. His kiss had left its mark on her senses, and on his. She knew what he wanted. It was there in the way he looked at her, in the way he held his shoulders and drew in a sharp breath. One word from her could make all the difference in the world. And no difference whatsoever.

They'd been down this road before, giving in to the physical aspect of their marriage time and time again. Six months apart had sharpened that need, but she didn't see how it could have changed all the reasons they had for separating. And it certainly hadn't changed the biggest reason of all.

Taking great care to tear her gaze away, she said, "Crystal, are you sure you don't mind showing Nick and Mertyl to their rooms?"

Crystal smiled down at Mertyl. "If Nick would be kind enough to help Mertyl and me up those tricky old stairs, we can handle the rest, can't we Mertyl?"

Mertyl continued to nod, but Nick ground his teeth so hard his jaw ached. The only room he wanted to be shown to, dammit, was Brittany's. There happened to be two very good reasons. One had to do with desire, the other with her safety. She would scoff at his mention of those two things in the same breath. When had one ever had anything to do with the other?

From his position he could see two of the four doors on this floor. He glanced over his shoulder where the open stairway stretched toward a dark upper level. He wondered if he would hear an intruder from that far away. And if he did, could he get down here and into Brittany's and Savannah's rooms in time?

"Come on, Nick," Crystal said shrewdly. "You're starting to look as green around the gills as poor Mertyl. Up we go."

Nick gave Brittany one last look, leaving her to make what

she wanted of his dark expression. No matter what she thought, things weren't over between them. They would talk again. Morning, noon and night if necessary. Maybe they had already tried to make their marriage work a hundred times. Somehow he had to convince her to try once more.

For now, he helped Crystal get the elderly lady into one of the bedrooms upstairs. The cat hissed at him for his trouble. Coming out of her stupor, Mertyl did the same, squinting up at him with distrust. "Who's he?" she asked Crystal.

"This is Nick Colter," Crystal said, turning back the blankets.

Clasping the lapels of her pink cardigan sweater tightly in one hand and holding her cat in the other, Mertyl still managed to point a shaking finger at Crystal. "I don't entertain strange men in my room, Missy, and neither should you."

Nick found himself backing from the room, Crystal right behind him. Laughing out loud, Crystal said, "Believe me, Mertyl, I'm with you."

The old lady gave Crystal a feeble good-night, glared at Nick and closed the door with a firm click. Within seconds a lock ground into place.

"Why, Nicky, I don't believe she trusts you."

Nick scowled. Nobody had called him Nicky since the third grade.

"Which room do you want to sleep in tonight?" Crystal asked. "Perhaps I should rephrase the question. Which room *upstairs?* You can have your choice of the three that aren't rented."

Nick stopped at the first door he came to. "Rented?"

Dropping a stack of blankets and sheets she'd taken from a hall closet into his hands, Crystal said, "Yes, rented. By boarders." At his blank expression, she said, "You might have noticed that motels aren't exactly popping up all over town. In fact, this is the only boarding house in Jasper Gulch. Didn't Brittany tell you she bought it?"

Now that Nick thought about it he remembered the old man

at the wedding reception saying something about a boarding house on Custer Street. But no, Brittany hadn't mentioned anything about the fact that she'd purchased it.

Suddenly the tedious twelve-hour drive from Chicago, the fear that came from looking over his shoulder and the seemingly impenetrable walls Brittany had erected converged into one huge knot between his shoulder blades. He really was exhausted, emotionally and physically. He needed a good night's sleep. The bedroom next to Mertyl's wasn't his first choice of places to spend the night, not by a long shot, but at least it was near the top of the stairs and within hearing distance of the first floor. Dropping the sheets and blankets over the iron bed frame, he turned around. He expected to find Crystal hovering nearby, but a quick glance in the hall found it empty.

Kneading the knot at the back of his neck, he closed the door and looked at his surroundings. The room could have come straight out of an old Western movie. The walls and ceiling were covered with faded wallpaper. The floor was hardwood, a throw rug the only thing covering the marred and scuffed surface. A lamp was perched on a painted bedside table, the only other furniture in the room a mismatched dresser and the double bed. He'd slept in a lot worse places, and supposed that for now any bed would do.

He was in the process of stuffing a pillow into a case when a knock sounded on the door behind him. Hope that it might be Brittany sprang out of nowhere, only to die at his first glimpse of blond hair instead of brown. Crystal shouldered her way into the room and dropped his duffel bag and suitcase on the floor.

With one eyebrow raised, she said, "Sorry to disappoint you."

The woman obviously read body language very well. Nick saw no sense in trying to explain, so he simply shrugged and said, "Thanks for bringing up my bags."

She turned to go. "Nick?" she said over her shoulder.

He shook the sheet out. Holding it in midair, he waited for her to continue.

"Brittany says good night."

His throat constricted and his eyes closed for a moment, the sheet falling to the bed. Crystal Galloway had a walk that could stop traffic, and probably had. She was unusual, to say the least. Instinct told him she would be a very loyal friend. He wasn't surprised Brittany had chosen her. His wife had always had very good taste in friends. He couldn't say the same for her taste in men.

"By the way," Crystal added, "don't be alarmed if you see a curtain flutter in the window across the street."

Nick came to full attention. Crystal, however, didn't appear to be the least bit concerned about being watched. Winking badly, she said, "Most of the old women in Jasper Gulch spend half the day on the phone and the other half spying on their neighbors. The eighty-one-year-old widow across the street is no exception. Mrs. Fergusson has a weak heart, so you'd better draw the shade. We wouldn't want her to see more than she bargained for now, would we?"

His jaw dropped in mild amazement. "The old lady in the next room locks her door because she doesn't trust me and the one across the street is a window peeper. It looks as if I'm going to have to be on my best behavior at every turn."

Easing out the door an inch at a time, Crystal said, "Something tells me your best behavior could be very dangerous to a woman who isn't immune. There's a bathroom at the end of the hall. Don't forget about your shade. Oh, and if it'll make you feel any better to rattle Mertyl's doorknob, be my guest."

Nick stared at the closed door for a full five seconds after she'd gone. Picking up where he'd left off with the sheet, he had an uncustomary urge to grin.

"A watched pot never boils, Savannah," Brittany whispered, turning on the tap at the kitchen sink.

Savannah held her position in the doorway where she had

a clear view of the living room sofa. "I'm not watching a pot. I'm watching Daddy. He looks different when he's sleeping."

Brittany waited until the coffeepot was filled with water before allowing herself to turn around. Savannah always rose before the crack of dawn, and today was no exception. She was wearing her favorite flannel nightgown and the fluffy moose slippers that made her feet look huge. It was still dark outside, but the kitchen light stretched into the next room, falling across the sofa where Nick was sleeping.

Brittany supposed Savannah was right. Nick *did* look different while he was sleeping. He was lying on his back, his feet hanging over one end of the sofa, Mertyl's cat sound asleep on his thighs. One of Nick's hands rested on the floor, the other arm was flopped over his head. His eyes were closed, his chest moving up and down with his even breathing. He should have looked completely at ease, devoid of all worry and tension. Only Nick Colter could look intense even in repose.

In the early years of their marriage she'd loved to watch him sleep. In those days they'd had a one-bedroom apartment that did little to keep out the sounds of faulty mufflers and hissing brakes and honking horns on the street below. While Savannah slept in her crib in the corner, Brittany would memorize her new husband's face. She used to smooth a fingertip over his brow, down the crease in one lean cheek and across the shallow cleft in his chin.

More often than not, he woke up. Finding her watching him, an entirely different intensity would enter his eyes.

She shook herself back to the present. Pouring the water into the coffee maker, she wondered when he'd crept down the stairs and crashed on her sofa. It must have been after she'd dropped off to sleep in the wee hours of the morning. Until then, she'd lain awake, thinking about the kiss he'd given her in the study and what had gone wrong in their marriage. She should have known by now that it was useless to try to pinpoint any one thing.

"When will he wake up?" Savannah asked.

"It's hard to say Savannah-banana."

The little girl giggled into her hand, a gesture she'd picked up from Haley Carson, one of the older girls she'd befriended at school. "That's what Daddy calls me."

When the coffee started dripping through the filter, Brittany set out a bowl, cup and spoon for Savannah's breakfast. While Savannah ate, Brittany put the oatmeal on for Mertyl and made the juice. Savannah was a chatterbox, but this morning she chattered in whispers, so as not to wake her father. Brittany helped herself to a cup of coffee, answering in whispers of her own. Taking that first sip, she looked at her child over the rim. Savannah was happy. Crystal claimed the child glowed. Brittany knew she'd done the right thing by moving to Jasper Gulch, even though the realization always left her feeling sad for what might have been.

Today Savannah was a bubbly, happy little girl. But for a year and a half Brittany had been afraid that Savannah would never be happy again. Her child had always been a light sleeper. One night almost two years ago she'd awakened in the night and had run screaming into Brittany's bed. Two burglars wearing ski masks had broken into their apartment. Nick had been on a stakeout, and for twenty terrifying minutes, Brittany hadn't known whether she and Savannah would survive the night. The only thing that had kept her from falling to pieces had been fear for Savannah's safety. The burglars finally left with eighty-three dollars in quarters Brittany had been saving, a radio and a ring that had belonged to her mother.

The marriage had been strained for a long time, but suddenly Savannah was afraid of her own shadow, and Nick blamed himself for not being there. As a cop, he'd always taken on the world's troubles and had tried to protect Brittany and Savannah from all of it. Arguing was nothing new to them, but their arguments took on a new dimension. Accusations and recriminations were hurtled in anger and couldn't be

taken back. Savannah's banshee screams became common-
place in the middle of the night. Nick had always been intense,
but this was different. He looked at her with guilt, making her
wonder if he'd ever really looked at her with love.

How many times had Brittany insisted that she could take
care of herself? How many times had Nick shouted that she
shouldn't have to? They yelled about things that weren't really
the issue, and never once mentioned the one thing that was.

And then, one day while she'd been rocking Savannah back
to sleep, she saw a magazine article about a little town in
South Dakota that was steadily losing all its women to the lure
of better job prospects in the cities. Brittany had scanned the
portion of the article about men who were shy but willing, her
eyes catching on a statement proclaiming that the biggest
crimes in Jasper Gulch were gossip and jaywalking.

Such a place had sounded like heaven, and seemed like an
answer to her prayers. She'd read the article over and over. A
few days later she'd shown it to Nick. She would never forget
the dull look in his eyes when she'd told him she wanted to
take Savannah and go there. She'd expected him to rant and
rave. She'd hoped he would beg her not to leave. Instead, he'd
turned his back to her and sighed. To Brittany, it had sounded
painfully like relief.

He'd uttered only one word. "When?"

Although she couldn't answer, that was the moment she'd
faced the fact that their marriage was finally over.

"Can I wake Daddy up?" Savannah asked, bringing Brittany back to the present.

Brittany looked into the shadows in the living room and
slowly shook her head. "Let him sleep a little longer. If he
hasn't opened his eyes by the time you're ready for church,
you can wake him then."

Nick didn't know where he was. His neck was stiff, his
back ached, and his legs were numb from the knees down. He

opened his eyes and turned his head and found himself staring into a pixie face three inches from his.

"Hi, Daddy."

"Morning." He raised his knees, which felt as if they weighed a hundred pounds apiece, and heard, more than saw, the big yellow cat plop to the couch and then to the floor, yowling at having his sleep interrupted. Within seconds the cat was curled into a ball, his eyes closed once again.

"Daisy snores," Savannah said seriously.

Eyeing the overweight cat, Nick thought it was aptly named. It was obviously more potted plant than pet.

"You sleep funny."

Nick sat up in a flash and grabbed Savannah by the waist, tickling her until she begged him to stop. When her shrieks died down, she reached a hand to his jaw. "And you need to shave."

Pressing his face into her hand and rubbing like sandpaper, he said, "When did you get so bossy? And I thought you were six, not sixty."

Savannah wrinkled her nose and giggled again. "That's what Mommy says."

"Where is your mommy?"

"I'm right here, Nick."

Brittany stepped into the room, her heels clicking on the hardwood floor. Nick rose to his feet just as Crystal traipsed by in a ratty bathrobe and slippers. "What's the matter?" the blonde asked. "Wasn't your bed comfortable?"

She disappeared into the kitchen about the same time Mertyl appeared at the top of the stairs. In a feeble, frail little voice, she said, "I haven't slept so well in years, but I must have a touch of the flu. Brittany, dear, where do you keep the aspirin?"

"They're in a childproof bottle in the medicine cabinet in the bathroom."

"If you need help opening it," Crystal called from the next room, "have Savannah help you."

"You don't have to yell, dear."

Nick settled his hands to his hips and studied the old woman. If Mertyl Gentry had the flu, he would be a good candidate for the priesthood.

Savannah skipped into the kitchen, and suddenly Brittany didn't appear to know where to look. Settling her gaze somewhere in the vicinity of his left shoulder, she said, "Savannah wanted to wake you, but I thought you needed your sleep. I've enrolled her in Miss Opal's Sunday school class. It begins in half an hour."

Nick rubbed the bleariness from his eyes. Last night he and Brittany had known a moment of passion, followed by a stretch of companionship, which had ended with a tense moment, during which she'd thrown up enough barriers to keep him firmly at bay. He'd spent a great deal of the night thinking about all three of those things, but his mind kept returning to the moment of passion.

He wanted to talk to her about their imminent divorce. Now he wondered if she was trying to make a statement with her black skirt and white sweater. Nothing had ever been black-and-white between them. Ever.

"You look nice," he said quietly.

Brittany squared her shoulders and straightened her back. She knew what Nick was doing. It just so happened that she knew what she had to do, too. She would simply get back on even footing where he was concerned. She would be hospitable, friendly, ex-wifely. She'd rehearsed what she was going to say before falling asleep last night and again this morning while she'd been getting dressed for church.

Her plans hadn't included training her eyes on Nick's bare feet and slowly working her way higher.

When they'd been married, he'd slept in the nude. This morning he wore black sweat pants that clung in places *ex*-wives had no business looking. His wrinkled T-shirt had probably been black a hundred washings ago. It was stretched taut over his chest and shoulders, fitting him like a second skin. His jaw was dark with whisker stubble, his lips parted slightly.

"Guess I'd better hop in the shower, huh?" he asked.

His eyes delved into hers, leaving little doubt that the only place he was thinking about hopping into was bed. With her.

Savannah and Crystal were talking, their voices a low murmur in the next room. It reminded Brittany that she had to put a stop to this. She couldn't harbor these fantasies every time he came to visit Savannah. And she wouldn't. "Nick."

"Hmm?" He took a step closer. "Oh, I hope you don't mind that I decided to bunk down on the couch. I have no idea how anybody can call the country quiet. Honking horns and sirens are nothing compared to all the sighing of the wind, the rattling of the shutters and the creaking and groaning and shifting of this old house."

"I'm sorry you didn't sleep well."

He held up one hand. "Hey, I'm explaining, not complaining. Guess I'd better go see about that shower. And I'd better unpack my razor. Savannah thinks I'll look better after I shave."

That proved to Brittany that little girls and grown women had entirely different opinions about what constituted a good-looking man. Nick had disappeared up the stairs before Brittany had realized he'd done it again. He'd taken her mind off what she was *supposed* to tell him and made her think about things she *wasn't* supposed to think about anymore.

She massaged her forehead, wondering if Mertyl had found the aspirin. She wasn't prone to headaches, but she felt one the size of Mount Rushmore coming on.

Raising her chin, she stared at the place Nick had slept. On second thought, she didn't need aspirin. All she needed was a brisk attitude and a firm resolve.

Brisk and firm, Brittany reminded herself, hurrying Savannah into her coat twenty minutes later. Brisk and firm.

Her decision to leave Nick six months ago hadn't been

made lightly. If he had beaten her or chased other women or been an ax murderer, leaving might have been easier. As it was, it had been the single most difficult thing she'd ever done. She and Nick were both to blame, she supposed, and they both had reasons for the things they'd done. She had Savannah to think about, her daughter's happiness and well-being much more important than the loneliness that had a way of slipping past Brittany's defenses when she least expected.

She should have anticipated the drowsy, hazy thoughts she was having, now that she'd seen Nick again. More than anything, she should have expected this yearning to see him smile—when she knew darn well that Nick Colter rarely smiled. Forewarned should have been forearmed, and might have been if he had arrived when he'd said he would. She supposed she should have expected that, too.

OK, he'd caught her off guard. But she'd recovered.

She didn't know why he was fiddling with the lock on the front door, and she didn't see any reason to ask. From now on she was going to keep a handle on her resolve. Brisk and firm.

"Hurry, Daddy," Savannah said. "Get your coat."

Nick's salute earned a giggle from Savannah and a brittle smile from Brittany. Nick didn't say a word as he retrieved his bomber jacket from the back of the sofa and followed them out the door, but he'd seen drill sergeants with less-intimidating posture than Brittany's.

They took her car, Savannah keeping up a steady stream of prattle all the way. The church sat on the corner of First and Church Streets. Like every other building in town, it could have used a coat of paint. Maybe that was part of its charm. Stained-glass windows gleamed in the morning sunshine, that same sun glinting off a white steeple high on the roof.

A group of women who were huddled on the steps looked up as he, Brittany and Savannah approached. "Morning, Miss Opal," Savannah called.

"Good morning," a short lady with a double chin called.

Pressing a hand to her forehead, she lowered her voice. "Some of the other children have already arrived. Why don't you go in and say hello?"

The moment Savannah disappeared through the double doors, another woman, this one tall and wearing a pinched expression, said, "I don't know whether you're aware, Brittany, but something dreadful happened at the wedding reception last night."

"Merciful heavens," the woman with the double chin interrupted, "something dreadful indeed. Why, somebody spiked the punch, and not one of the fine members of the Ladies Aid Society caught it until it was too late."

The four other gray-haired women standing on the steps nodded their heads. Grimacing at the sudden movement, they placed a hand to their foreheads. The tall, skinny one said, "We're calling a special meeting this afternoon during which we'll try to recount the events leading to such a dreadful act. Perhaps someone saw something or someone."

Nick knew the moment he came under suspicion. The leader of the group narrowed her eyes and pursed her lips. "I don't believe we've met."

Brittany made short work of the introductions. When she was finished, Isabell Pruitt, the tall, skinny one who bore a striking resemblance to Olive Oyl, gave Nick a critical squint and said, "And what time did you arrive at the reception, Mr. Colter?"

Nick lifted one foot to the bottom step and smiled up at the woman. "I'm afraid I got there just about the time you fine ladies decided to do the Bunny Hop."

All six of the women exchanged pained looks.

"Isabell," Brittany said quietly, "it's good to see you and Opal speaking again."

"Yes," Isabell said, nodding carefully. "We've decided to let bygones be bygones. And I must say our united front couldn't have come at a more crucial time."

Nodding gravely, Opal said, "The meeting will begin at

one, Brittany. You're more than welcome to join us. Were you planning to help in my class again this morning?''

Nick shook his head before Brittany could open her mouth. ''Sorry, but Brittany's been itching to give me a piece of her mind ever since I arrived. First things first, you know?''

''Yes, yes, of course,'' Opal muttered. ''By all means, first things first.''

Brittany didn't have the presence of mind to clamp her mouth shut until after the six staunchest members of the Jasper Gulch Ladies Aid Society had gone inside. Even then she stared at Nick for a full five seconds before she had formed a coherent thought. ''What on earth possessed you to tell them that?''

''It's true, isn't it?''

''So?''

''So,'' he answered, looking far too sure of himself for her peace of mind, ''go ahead. Tell me whatever it is you're so hell-bent to say. But you might as well know right now that I intend to change your mind about the divorce.''

The church bell rang, another gong keeping perfect time inside Brittany's head. When it was quiet again, she said, ''What are you talking about?''

He placed his foot back on the sidewalk and turned to face her. His movements were fluid, the expression in his blue eyes far more serious than she'd expected. ''I'm talking about you and me and the feelings that are still between us. I'm talking about in sickness and in health, in good times and in bad. But wait, don't let me do all the talking. There's something you want to say. You might as well say it while we walk.''

''You want to take a walk?''

''Yeah. I want to take a walk. Better yet, I want to play hookey. When was the last time you played hookey, Brittany?''

Brittany might have been able to resist the invitation in the depths of Nick's eyes, but she couldn't resist the challenge in his voice as he said, "What's the matter? Don't you trust yourself to be alone with me for five minutes?"

She shoved her hands into her coat pockets and hurried after him. "You're something else, Nick Colter, do you know that?"

"Yeah, I know."

"If you know, what makes you so sure I'll walk with you?"

He was walking fast, and she was getting winded trying to keep up with him. He slowed down long enough to slip an arm around her back and steer her across the street. "Because I'm adorable?"

"You are *not* adorable."

"Oh, really?" he asked quietly. "Why don't you tell me how you'd describe me."

Brittany removed her hands from her pockets and looked around. They had entered the alley that ran behind the stores on the east side of Main Street. Today was Sunday, and all the businesses were closed. Even the diner shut down one day a week, which meant that nobody was out and about. Except her and Nick.

Her heels clicked on the uneven, packed ground. Beside her, Nick's footsteps were silent. The wind couldn't reach them here in the alley. Without it the sun felt blessedly warm. It melted snow off rooftops, droplets of water clinging to the pointy tips of icicles before plopping into puddles like the first music of spring.

"Well?" Nick asked, their steps slowing, then stopping completely near the diner's back door.

She wished she could blame the excitement inching through her veins on spring fever. But Nick wasn't the only one who never lied. Unfortunately, there was more to the sighing of her heart than a change of seasons.

How would she describe him? she thought, staring up at him. This close he was very intimidating. And very handsome. He could torture her from now until eternity, but she'd never admit that out loud.

He moved without making a sound, his voice a husky baritone as he said, "What are you thinking?"

"I...never mind."

He leaned toward her, his face inches from hers. "I think you're thinking the same thing I'm thinking. That a kiss would be heaven and a warm bed even better."

"That isn't what I was thinking. At least not exactly," she whispered, her eyes on his as he drew closer.

"Then what, exactly?"

His mouth brushed the corner of her lips, his breath warm on her skin. Her eyes fluttered closed when his lips moved over half an inch. "You're a bully," she whispered.

He kissed the indentation above her upper lip. "And?"

"And you're too good-looking for your own good."

"Is that anything like being adorable?"

His mouth covered hers like it had countless times before. His breathing became ragged, his kiss insistent. He slipped his arms around her back and pulled her tight to him, letting her know how much he wanted her.

In the darkest recesses of her mind, Brittany knew this wasn't what she'd come here to do. But it had been so long since she'd felt this way, so long since she'd been giddy with anticipation and excitement, drunk on dreams and on desire. She tried to remind herself of the problems they'd had during their six-and-a-half-year marriage, but it wasn't easy to remember her quiet hopelessness when Nick was kissing her and touching her, when he felt so good and smelled so good.

Nick heard Brittany's sigh, saw her smile, felt her shudder. Sweet heaven. That's what she was, what she'd always been. She was slender and soft as only a woman could be, pliant and aggressive in a way that was uniquely her own. It was a potent combination, and had him needing, seeking...more.

He opened his eyes for but an instant, just long enough to catch a movement at the very edge of his peripheral vision. He swung around, all his senses on red alert.

Brittany gasped for air and staggered. She hadn't heard any

sound, but before she could blink there was a scuffle and a grunt as Nick pinned a man against the building in the alley.

The man groaned. "What the—".

"All right," Nick ground out, his mouth mere inches from the other man's ear. "Who are you and what the hell are you doing here?"

Chapter Three

"**O**h, my goodness! What are you doing? Let him go!"

Nick felt a series of tugs on his arm. Glancing over his shoulder, he saw a woman with long, wavy brown hair and eyes gone huge with fear. "You know this man?"

She nodded, a blush creeping up her face. In a glance Nick noted that she was wearing a long bathrobe, its pale blue color in stark contrast to the embarrassment tingeing her neck. Beneath the blush he could see the marks a man's whisker stubble had left on her sensitive skin.

The man he had pinned against the building had plenty of whisker stubble. Brown whisker stubble. Now that Nick took the time to notice, the color of the man's hair was brown, too. Brown, not gray. Certainly not silver.

Damn. He'd overreacted.

He released the other man and instantly took a backward step. Adrenaline still pumped through his veins, frustration close on its heels. Since anger was the quickest way to vent it, Nick squeezed his hands into fists at his sides and sputtered, "Who are you? And what the hell are you doing here?"

The man pushed himself away from the building, his own

hands curling into fists. "My name's Burke Kincaid. I ran out of gas just outside of town last night, so I hiked in. Nobody was around except L— er, Miss Graham, so she helped me. Now who the hell are you?"

Everything had happened so fast Brittany was having difficulty taking it all in. One moment Nick had been kissing her, and the next thing she knew he had a man pressed up against a building. Although she'd never seen him before, she could tell from the integrity in his eyes that Burke Kincaid was an innocent man. He was also an angry man. Rightly so.

She happened to glance at Louetta Graham. An instant later Louetta met her gaze. Brittany had never seen Louetta with her hair down, and certainly never in slippers and a robe and not much else. Suddenly, everything she'd heard about Louetta flashed through her mind. The other woman was painfully shy, and very kind. Several months ago she'd gone to work for Melody Carson in the town's only diner. With Melody due to have a baby soon, Louetta practically ran the place single-handedly. She still blushed every time one of the local boys made a pass at her, but the few times Brittany had heard Louetta laugh, she'd stopped and stared, because hers wasn't the laughter a person would associate with a woman who'd been voted "The girl most likely not to" by her graduating class.

Evidently Louetta's graduating class had been wrong.

Her hair was mussed, and her mouth had obviously been very thoroughly kissed recently. Brittany wet her own lips, thinking the same could be said for her. Which brought Brittany's gaze back to Nick. She recognized the anger in his features and in the way he squeezed his fingers into fists at his sides. She also recognized the fear beneath the anger. That, she didn't understand.

"I'm Nick Colter. Brittany's husband." He scooped the man's cowboy hat off the ground and handed it over. "Sorry. I thought you were somebody else."

The other man accepted the hat but not the apology. "It seems to me your hello could use a little work."

Nick nodded, the small gesture an acknowledgment of fault and an admission to an error in judgment. He would have said more, but it was pretty difficult to make amends with a man who was wearing paint chips on one side of his face.

Burke Kincaid couldn't have been more than a few years older than Nick, but something about the steadiness of his gaze reminded Nick of his father. "Now, Nicholas," Joe Colter used to say. "Your mother and I aren't raising any hotheads. Wild animals get mad. People get angry. If you're angry, take it out on that stack of wood out back."

Nick had split a lot of wood in his day.

Sometimes his mother had brought him out something cool to drink. More often than not she'd stuck around, stacking the wood he'd split, her hands work-roughened and chapped, her face bearing far too many lines for a woman her age.

"Everyone's born with gifts," Clarice would say, staring at the house with its peeling paint and sagging roof. "Money doesn't happen to be one of ours. But pride is one of your greatest strengths, Nicholas, and so is brawn, neither of which amounts to a hill of beans unless you have the brains to back them up."

Nick shook his head at the memory. Watching as Burke strode in the direction of the town's only gas station and Louetta disappeared inside the door that led to the apartment over the diner, he wondered how many times he'd allowed anger to get in the way of his brain.

Patting the revolver underneath his coat, he took a deep breath, released it and took another before turning to face Brittany. Her arms were crossed, her shoulders set, her eyes wary. His rough handling hadn't done any lasting damage to Burke Kincaid, but it had raised Brittany's suspicion.

She stared at him, unblinking, the only sound that of droplets of water plopping into puddles on the ground. Finally she said, "Why did you come here, Nick?"

Brittany saw Nick take a step toward her, only to stop abruptly as if he'd thought better of coming any closer. His chest expanded with the deep breath he took, his fingers raking through his hair. "Everything I've told you is true. I want you and Savannah to move back to Chicago with me. If you won't do that, I'd like you both to stay with my parents in Florida for a while."

She took a moment to digest the information he'd given her. The man standing before her wasn't an awkward cowboy wearing scuffed boots and a bolo tie. He was an intimidating man in jeans and a worn bomber jacket. He was five foot eleven and three-quarter inches tall. The lack of that last quarter inch had always rankled him. Some men would have considered it close enough and called themselves an even six feet. But not Nick.

Nicholas Colter was a lot of things. Egotistical, overbearing and stubborn to name a few. But he never lied. That didn't mean he always told the complete truth. At least not until he had to.

Glancing at the footsteps Burke Kincaid had left in the snow when Nick had hauled him up against the building without warning, she said, "Why, Nick?"

He narrowed his eyes as if waiting for her to be a little more specific. That expression could raise her hackles faster than anything else. Today she wasn't giving in to it, not until she had some answers.

Glancing in both directions in the back alley, she pulled her coat closer to her body and crossed her arms. "Why did you come to Jasper Gulch? Why did you show up two days early? Why did you shove an innocent man up against a wall? And why do you want Savannah and me to pay your parents a visit?"

"That's a lot of whys, even for you."

"That's not an answer."

She followed the course of his gaze up to the second-story

window where Louetta now lived. "Have you ever seen that man before?" he asked.

Brittany shook her head.

"Do you believe his story about running out of gas?"

Her gaze trailed slowly back to his. "Don't you?"

Nick ran a hand through his hair, scrubbed it over his forehead, down his face. Kincaid's story wouldn't have been hard to check out, but the truth was Nick believed it. The problem he was having wasn't with the other man's story. Jasper Gulch didn't have much more than five hundred residents. Brittany had been here nearly six months, yet she'd never seen Burke Kincaid. That meant that Nick wasn't the only man who'd slipped into town undetected last night. The thought turned his stomach.

A sense of dread dogged his every thought. He had to tell Brittany what was going on. Imposing an iron will upon himself, he met her unwavering gaze and said, "I'll tell you everything. In order to do that, there's something I have to show you." He glanced at his watch. "What time do we have to pick up Savannah from Sunday school?"

Brittany glanced at her own watch. "In half an hour."

"That doesn't leave us a lot of time. Where are your car keys?"

She took them out of her pocket.

Snatching them from her palm, he said, "I'll get the car. Wait right here."

Nick hurried through the alley the way he'd come. Within minutes, he squealed around the corner in her car, slamming to a stop a foot away from where she stood. She jerked the door open and climbed in. Neither of them said a word during the short drive to her place on Custer Street.

Since he'd always believed that actions spoke louder than words, he pulled a sharp object from his pocket and deftly picked the poor excuse for a lock she had on her front door. Her key clinked when she dropped it, unused, back into her purse, but she didn't say a word. He ushered her inside. Kicking the door shut behind them, he waited for her to face him. And then he said, "Dawson's back on the street."

Brittany took a quick, sharp breath, halted as much by the tone of Nick's voice as by the words he'd uttered. She shivered at the mention of Dawson's name, the instinctive reaction one of derision followed closely by fear. She'd never seen Kipp Dawson in person, but she'd seen his picture in the newspaper. Even in the grainy photo, his leer had been sinister, the curl of his lip calculating and cold. Although he was only in his mid-thirties, his hair was completely gray. People on both sides of the law shuddered at the mention of the Silver Fox. He was suspected of having his hand in some of the worst illegal pots in Chicago. Drugs, prostitution, extortion. Over the years his victims had gotten younger and younger, the police more desperate to nail his coffin shut, or at the very least throw him behind bars and leave him there. Nick had been instrumental in Dawson's capture, his testimony the deciding factor in the jury's guilty verdict.

"I thought the judge gave him fifteen to twenty years," Brittany said.

"His attorneys found a loophole. Hell, they probably paid off a witness. Or a judge. Anyway, the case was appealed, the sentence overturned. Dawson's out."

Brittany closed her eyes, the caption beneath that grainy newspaper photo flashing through her mind. "Dawson maintains innocence. Demands formal apology from cop who arrested him."

That cop had been Nicholas Colter.

The thought of what such a man might do to Nick made Brittany nauseous. She'd always hated living with the cold knot of fear for Nick's life. She still hated it. Separated or divorced, she knew she always would. But she didn't understand what Kipp Dawson had to do with her stay in Jasper Gulch.

"Have you seen him?" she asked, studying every subtle nuance of Nick's expression.

He shook his head only once.

"But you've heard from him?"

A bead of sweat ran down the side of Nick's face. He unzipped his coat and deftly removed it. "Yeah. I've heard from him."

Without waiting for Brittany to follow, he strode to the open stairway. He sensed more than saw her unbutton her own coat, and heard her footsteps on the stairs. Striding directly into the room he'd chosen last night, he yanked an old suitcase from underneath the bed. The mechanism was rusty. Impatient, he twisted it so hard it broke, but the latch creaked open. He rummaged through the bottom of the suitcase, pulling out a manila envelope bearing a Chicago postmark and Nick's name and address in neatly printed letters.

Brittany noticed the quiver in Nick's hand when he gave her the envelope. Inside was a copy of an article that had run in one of the largest women's magazines in the country. The folks of Jasper Gulch had had great fun when the story about the women who had come to the town dubbed "Bachelor Gulch" had come out a few months ago. Savannah had taken the magazine to school for show and tell, proudly pointing to the picture of her and Brittany, along with the handful of other new "gals" who'd moved to Jasper Gulch.

Brittany raised the article closer to her face. She recognized it, all right. One copy was hanging on the wall in the Clip & Curl, another in the diner. There was one difference. Those glossy pages didn't have a circle and two cross hairs drawn around her and Savannah.

The article in her hand did.

Fear, stark and vivid, took hold of her vocal cords. Swallowing tightly, she could manage only one word. "Savannah."

She began to pace, the action helping to keep up with all her questions, all the denials that sprang into her mind. "I brought Savannah here because it's supposed to be a safe place. I mean, most people don't even lock their doors here."

Remembering the way he'd so effortlessly picked the lock in her front door, she swung around. "Do you really think it's necessary that I leave? How can I? I bought this house with the money my father left me. For the first time in my life I'm putting down roots. Savannah's happy here. And I think I could be."

Nick didn't know what to say. Mention of Brittany's father reminded him of everything he'd done wrong where she was concerned. Ten years ago she'd been nothing like the girls who'd normally caught his eye. It was as if a bolt of lightning had come out of nowhere, striking him where he'd stood. Brittany hadn't had a chance after that. Her father had done everything in his power to end the relationship. He'd even sent Brittany away for an entire summer. When she got back she was eighteen, and the attraction between her and Nick was stronger than ever.

Back then, Nick hadn't much cared for Samuel Matthews. Now that he had a daughter of his own, Nick had a little more empathy for what the man had gone through. A high-level executive in great demand, Sam had moved often, taking his family with him all over the country. Brittany's mother had died two years before Nick had come into the picture. Brittany's older sister had already been a biochemist out East, her older brother well on his way to becoming a talented surgeon in California. Brittany would have finished college, too, if a boy from the wrong side of the tracks with a chip on his shoulder hadn't intervened.

Brittany had claimed they were like Romeo and Juliet and were destined to be together. Nick had only known he couldn't stop thinking about her. She'd brought out every masculine impulse he'd ever had. He'd wanted to make love to her. Even more, he'd wanted to take care of her and keep her safe.

He'd done one helluva job of that.

First he'd gotten her pregnant. Then he hadn't been there when two punks in ski masks had broken into their apartment in the middle of the night two years ago. And now this.

"Nick?"

He stared wordlessly at her, his heart pounding. The papers crinkled in her hand when she lifted them, her voice shaking. "How can you be sure this came from Dawson?"

Nick kneaded the back of his neck. Call it intuition. Call it gut instinct. Call it fear. A primitive warning had sounded in his head the instant he'd pulled that article out of the envelope five days ago. The warning had been beeping like a blip of radar ever since. He turned the envelope over in Brittany's hand, staring at the perfect handwriting on the label. Kipp Dawson had been meticulous right down to the tips of his expensive Italian shoes. It might have been a coincidence that Nick had learned of Dawson's early release a week before. It might have been a coincidence that he'd reportedly been seen getting into a limousine in front of the police station where Nick worked in Chicago. Any seasoned cop would tell you there was no such thing as coincidence.

Since downplaying the seriousness of this situation would only make things worse, he said, "We'll only be sure if you or Savannah find yourselves staring down the barrel of Dawson's gun. By then it will be too late."

She ran her fingers through her hair, the action drawing wispy tendrils off her forehead. Without hair around her face, her eyes looked larger, her skin pale. Nick hated himself for doing this to her.

"I need time to think," she said. Glancing at the slender watch on her wrist, she said, "It's almost time to pick Savannah up from Sunday school."

"I'll go." At the wariness in her eyes, he said, "I promised her I'd spend the day with her. Besides, I'll feel better if I can keep an eye on her. Not that you haven't done a good job keeping her safe. It's just—"

"It's all right, Nick. I understand. Go ahead. Pick her up. Spend some time with her. I'll feel better knowing she's with you, too."

"I'd feel better if you'd come along."

He heard her sigh from twelve feet away. She shook her head. "I'm going to stay here and think. Don't worry, I'll be on the lookout for silver hair."

A noose wouldn't have left him in more need of air. "I'm sorry, Brittany."

"Don't be. This isn't your fault."

Nick reached for his jacket and put it on. Unable to meet Brittany's gaze, he turned on his heel and strode out the door. The logical part of his brain told him she was right. This wasn't his fault. It was all completely out of his control and had been from the very beginning. The part of him reacting to primitive fear for Brittany's and Savannah's lives told him something else entirely.

"Are you going to tell me what's on your mind or are you going to make me guess?"

Brittany glanced up from the coffee she was stirring, straight into exotic green eyes. "What makes you think something's bothering me?"

Crystal Galloway made a most unbecoming and unfeminine sound. "Oh, I don't know. Maybe it has something to do with the fact that you just put about sixteen teaspoons of sugar into my coffee, and I only take cream."

Biting her lip, Brittany carried the cup to the sink and promptly dumped its contents down the drain.

"Also," Crystal continued from her position at the oak table, "you didn't go to church today. You got dressed for it, but you didn't go. It doesn't take a genius to recognize your symptoms. You've got man trouble written all over you."

Brittany turned around. Crossing her ankles, she leaned her back against the cabinet behind her and studied her friend. Crystal rarely went to church on Sundays, preferring to stay in her robe until noon, at least. She said it wasn't that she thought it was mumbo-jumbo. It was just that she'd studied the Bible so extensively the average preacher couldn't make her think. And that was a preacher's job, she'd said. To save souls and to make people think.

Crystal Galloway was too smart for her own good.

"Well?" she asked, propping her feet on a nearby chair. "Would you mind bringing me another cup of coffee? As long as you're up and all?"

She was also sarcastic and, on Sunday mornings at least, she was as lazy as Mertyl's big, yellow cat.

Brittany filled a second cup with the steaming liquid. Opening the refrigerator, she added a generous helping of cream. Handing the cup to Crystal, she sank into a nearby chair and quietly said, "I know why Nick came to Jasper Gulch."

Crystal took a sip of coffee. "There's more behind his arrival than meets the eye?"

Brittany mimicked Crystal's earlier unbecoming sound. There was always more to Nick than met the eye. There was always something behind the hint of his smile, the gleam of interest in his eyes and the display of impatience in his movements. Oh, the man wanted her. On a physical level, he always had. She didn't doubt that he'd missed her and Savannah, but the real reason he'd come here had been to protect them from harm. Not to see them. Certainly not to try to convince her to give their marriage another chance. Although he probably wanted those things, they weren't the main reasons he'd come.

The main reason behind everything Nick did was his sense of responsibility. He'd considered it his responsibility to marry her when she'd been pregnant with Savannah. He'd considered it his responsibility to provide for them. Now he considered it his responsibility to keep them safe.

Responsibility was Nick Colter's middle name.

"Were you planning to tell me why Nick came to Jasper Gulch, Brittany? Or did you just want me to know that you know?"

Brittany looked into Crystal's green eyes. Smoothing her fingertip along the rim of her cup, she said, "He thinks Savannah and I are in danger."

"What kind of danger?"

Brittany's fingertip stilled, her voice becoming a whisper. "Grave danger."

Crystal sat up straighter. Reaching across the table, she laid a hand on Brittany's arm. "I think you'd better start at the beginning."

Brittany wasn't entirely certain where the beginning was, but she drew strength from her friend's warm touch, and told the story as best she could. She highlighted the events leading to Dawson's trial, touching upon some of the risks Nick took, omitting others. Crystal asked questions now and then, but for the most part she remained silent, absorbing everything she heard. Brittany couldn't blame her for her occasional gasps and the anything but subtle lift of her eyebrows. Brittany had lived it, and she was having a hard time believing that all the events were real.

"Then this vile man, this Kipp Dawson, is using you and Savannah to get even with Nick."

"There's no way to be sure, but that's what Nick believes."

Crystal was quiet for a moment, the intelligence in her eyes belying the image her rumpled bathrobe and uncombed hair portrayed. "Do you trust Nick's judgment, Brittany?"

Brittany gave the question a great deal of thought. Her instinctive response was yes. She trusted Nick's judgment. At least when it came to hardened criminals and the law. She trusted him to do his best and try his hardest to keep her and Savannah safe. After all, Nick had a sense of loyalty and responsibility that few mere mortals would attempt to carry alone. She'd once looked up the word *responsibility* in the dictionary. There were several definitions. Her least favorite was *burden*.

She'd never wanted to be a burden to him. Yet that's how she'd felt. At first, she hadn't understood what the strange, lost, dissatisfied feelings that had sneaked into her life had meant. During the last two years of her marriage, they'd become her constant companions. Discontent. Disillusionment.

The painful admission and day-to-day acceptance that Nick had married her because he'd had to. To a man like Nick, that was a good enough reason. To Brittany, the knowledge ate away at her composure and her feelings of self-worth.

She rose to her feet, walked to the sink, spun around. No. That was before she'd taken charge, taken control of her life, of her future, and of Savannah's. She was no longer an unsure young girl, hopelessly in love with a boy who was a clear study of someone motivated by ambition and overloaded with good intentions. She was no longer the victim of a shotgun wedding, of a marriage based on responsibility and strong attraction and, for Nick, at least, the need to prove himself over and over again. She refused to be a victim of anything. Or anyone.

What about Savannah's safety? whispered through her mind.

She walked over to the table. Pressing her palms to the smooth surface, she looked Crystal in the eye and said, "There are two things about Nick I'd stake my life on. One is his sense of direction. The man has never been lost in his life. The other is his gut instinct concerning criminals and how their minds work. It's almost as if he can smell danger, and hear it, and feel it. That sixth sense of his has saved his life on more than one occasion."

Crystal raised one delicately arched eyebrow. "I once read that people who have an extraordinary sense of direction have unusual amounts of iron deposits in the tips of their noses."

It took Brittany a moment to register the unexpected bit of trivia. Crystal shrugged one shoulder and smiled sheepishly. "Just thought I'd share my wealth of knowledge with you."

Crystal's exaggerated wink had the desired effect on Brittany. She released a huff of air that was part laugh, part exasperation. "Okay, Miss Fountain of Information," she began, "how would you classify Nick's gut instincts?"

Crystal's expression turned serious. "Those are more difficult to explain and even harder to dismiss. What are you going to do?''

''I don't want to leave Jasper Gulch, but I don't know what to do. Remember all the stories we've heard about how dead set Isabell Pruitt and the other members of the Ladies Aid Society were against advertising for women in the first place? 'Women of ill repute,' Isabell had proclaimed, 'that's the kind of women who will come to our fine, peaceful town. Ill will come of this. Mark my words.' How can I put her life, and everyone else's life, in danger?''

''*You're* not putting anybody's life in danger, Brittany. If this Dawson character is real, and if he chooses to come here, *he's* the one who will be responsible for that.''

''Then you think I should stay?''

''I think it's up to you. If he really has the connections you say he has, what makes you think he couldn't find you no matter where you are? I don't think you should let some criminal rob you of your town and your peace of mind. And I'm not so sure you should rule out a reconciliation with Nick. That man *wants* you. I can think of worse fates than being under his protection. But then, his protection isn't all you want, is it?''

Brittany straightened and crossed her arms. ''How did you get so smart?''

Crystal rolled her green eyes expressively. ''All my degrees should account for something.''

''How many degrees do you have, anyway?''

Crystal took her time rising to her feet. With a shrug she ambled toward the door, mumbling, ''I forget.''

Sure, Brittany thought to herself while she rinsed out the coffee cups. Crystal forgets. Pigs could fly. And being *wanted* by Nick and being protected by him might someday be enough.

''Daddy, what's your favorite color?''

Nick pulled his attention from the doorway and glanced at

the desk where Savannah was coloring. The child was on a roll, and had been asking questions all day. His favorite color? "Oh, I don't know," he said. "It's been a long time since I've thought about it."

He heard the sound of Brittany's voice. A quick glance in the other direction almost gave him whiplash, but it awarded him a glimpse of short, dark hair before she disappeared into the next room.

"Brown," he said. The color of Brittany's hair and eyes.

He had his second choice all ready, in case his little girl wanted to know. A close tie would have been blue—the color of Savannah's eyes and the denim jumper and ruffled shirt she was wearing right now.

Of course, Savannah didn't ask. She never asked questions he was prepared to answer. His little girl was something else. Good Lord she was bright. Oh sure, all parents thought their children were gifted. His daughter also happened to be exceptionally talkative.

He'd missed her. Seeing her today, he'd realized just how much. She chattered a mile a minute, pointing out things as if she were the adult and he the child. Nick didn't mind. He loved listening to her, loved the way her mind worked. More than anything he loved the fact that she seemed to have completely forgotten her fear and the nightmares she'd started having two years ago.

"Brown?" Savannah looked up at him with eyes very much like his own. "Most of the kids at school like blue and red. Haley Carson's favorite color is black. She's nine," she added, as if that explained everything.

Nodding, Nick looked out the window. The sun had shrunk the layer of snow blanketing the area. Now that darkness had fallen, it was impossible to tell how much. Even though it was now officially April, the weatherman was predicting temperatures to fall below the freezing mark before dawn.

True to his word, he'd spent most of the day with Savannah. They'd taken a walk, tried to build a snowman, played hide and seek. While Savannah had hidden in a closet upstairs, Nick had checked out the rest of this old relic. His first impression of the house had been pretty accurate. The place was huge and had all the security of a chicken coop.

Aside from that, he understood why Brittany liked it. She'd always dreamed of living in a big white house with a picket fence and a comfortable front porch. There was no picket fence, but the rest of this place fit the bill. Although most of the furniture had come with the house, Brittany's touches were everywhere. Two of the windowsills were lined with transparent vases in nearly every color of the rainbow. Pink hyacinths bloomed atop a pale blue cylinder-shaped vase. Purple crocuses blossomed in a lavender vase shaped like an hourglass. There were daffodils and tulips, and sprigs of white flowers he couldn't name, all blooming in see-through vases of pink and baby blue, spring green and butter yellow. Winter may have had a hold of the great outdoors, but here inside, Brittany had turned it into spring.

Brittany. How many times had her name crept into his thoughts today? How many times had she failed to meet his gaze?

He was waiting for her answer to a very important question. Although she hadn't told him what she'd decided to do, she didn't appear to be getting ready to pack. She and Crystal were making popcorn right now, the smell wafting all the way to the doctor's study where Savannah was coloring and talking, both at the same time.

"Haley used to live with her mom in Texas. Is Texas far away, Daddy?"

Nick nodded.

"As far as Chicago?"

"A little farther, I suppose."

Savannah chewed on that for a moment. "Haley says I'm kinda little to play with, but she likes talking to me. She got in trouble last summer for stealing cookies and stuff off her aunt's porch. She didn't hafta go to jail, though. Haley's not afraid of anything. She even went skinny-dipping with a boy. Her daddy sure was mad. Miss Isabell blamed her for stealing underwear off Lisa McCully's clothesline, too.'' Savannah giggled into her hand at the thought. Turning serious, she said, "Haley says she didn't do it, an' I believe her.''

A sound near the doorway drew Nick's gaze. "Savannah," Brittany asked, "are you talking your father's ears off?''

The child grinned. "Nope, he's still got both of them, see?''

Brittany gave Savannah an indulgent smile. "Crystal's putting the butter on the popcorn right now. I bet she could use your help.''

Savannah twirled to her feet like a forest sprite, her long fine hair billowing out behind her in the breeze she created. When she was out of sight, Brittany said, "She's had a good day today.''

Nick knew Brittany was including his participation in her assessment of Savannah's day. He settled his hands comfortably on his hips, cocked his head at a lofty angle and said, "I had more fun than she did. You were right about her. She *is* doing great. Although I have to tell you I'm a little concerned about her choice of friends.''

"You mean Haley Carson?'' she asked, strolling into the room.

"Is that kid for real?''

She smiled. "Don't worry, Nick. Haley's calmed down a lot since her father married Melody McCully.''

"I can't help worrying, Brittany.''

He watched her smile fade away, only to be replaced by an expression he liked a lot less. "Have you decided what you're going to do?'' he asked.

She nodded. "I'm not leaving.''

"Why the hell not?''

She cast him a carefully schooled look. "Being overbearing isn't going to help. If you would be patient for another minute, I'll try to explain my decision to you.''

Raking his fingers through his hair he supposed he could

see how Brittany might have thought that had sounded a little overbearing and impatient. But dammit to hell, what did she expect?

Although she'd raised her chin as if she was trying to be calm, he could see he'd made her angry. It was in her voice as she said, "If Dawson wants to find me, he will. No matter where I go. At least out here in this quiet little town we might see him coming."

Nick shook his head, thinking he'd liked her a lot better in the old days when he used to be able to talk her into bed, or anything else for that matter. He stopped pacing. That wasn't entirely true. Brittany had always teasingly called him a bully. And he had to admit he'd liked bullying her with his kisses. She'd always been a spitfire, a challenge. God, he'd loved to smooth a hand down her back and feel her resolve soften, to kiss the pout off her lips and the anger out of the rest of her.

She may not have been out-and-out furious right now, but she was plenty agitated. She'd started to pace, talking as she went. "We're going to have to tell the people in Jasper Gulch something. Although I have no idea what that should be." She stopped long enough to face him. "I suppose we could say, 'Excuse me. I don't want to alarm you, but a hardened criminal might be dropping by. Just thought you'd want to know. Bu-bye.'"

She started pacing again. Staring after her, he realized she'd acquired a lot of strength these past six months. He had to admit he liked it. He didn't even mind her sarcasm. And he was downright proud of her bravery. He only hoped it didn't get her killed.

Chest heaving, she turned to face him once again. "At the very least they're going to want to know how long you plan to stay. You're the police officer, Nick. You're the one with all the experience with bad guys and bad situations. What do you suggest we tell the innocent citizens of Jasper Gulch?"

He took one step toward her. Somewhere in the big house

a cat meowed and a little girl laughed. Ou… howled.

In the tiny room that had once been a doctor's stud… planted his feet firmly on the floor and quietly said, "We c… d tell them we've decided to give our marriage another chance."

Chapter Four

Brittany supposed she shouldn't have been surprised Nick had suggested they tell people they'd decided to give their marriage another try. He'd insinuated as much last night. But then he'd sat forward, his hands folded, his expression earnest, his body language screaming with intensity. Then, she'd seen it coming. Tonight he'd spoken so calmly he could have been asking what was for supper.

Tonight, she didn't know what to say.

The topic of their relationship and imminent divorce was certainly nothing new. They'd discussed every angle imaginable countless times in the past. Oh, it usually started innocently enough, him asking a question or her making a comment. Before they knew it their words would take on an impatient edge. They would begin to pace, their voices gaining volume.

Strangely, neither of them were pacing tonight. Nick appeared calm and in control. He wasn't pushing her or rushing her or bullying her. Instead, he was waiting patiently for her response. Maybe they'd both changed a little these past six months.

But tell people they were reconsidering their decision to divorce?

"You would lie?" she asked.

A muscle worked in his cheek, letting her know he wasn't as calm as he would have liked her to believe. "It wouldn't have to be a lie, Brittany."

He stepped in front of the desk lamp, his shadow flickering on the wall behind him as he strolled closer, his gaze steadily probing hers. The lighting accented the planes and hollows in his face, the squint lines beside his eyes, the leanness of his features. The past six months had left their mark on him. They'd been hard on her, too. In fact, leaving him had been the most difficult thing she'd ever done. There had been times when she'd thought she wouldn't make it through, when she'd awakened in a cold sweat, night after night. Heart racing, she'd wondered if she could handle living without him. The uncertainties had been paralyzing, the loneliness even worse. She never wanted to go through that again.

On second thought, the fact that neither of them were yelling didn't really change anything. It didn't change the problems they'd had in their marriage. It didn't change what they'd done, what they'd said. It certainly didn't change who they were. The funny thing was that Brittany didn't want Nick to change, at least not completely. She'd fallen in love with him when she'd been seventeen. Staring into his eyes, she realized that hadn't changed, either.

"It isn't like you to be this quiet," Nick said, taking another step toward her. "What's the matter, Daisy got your tongue?"

She shook her head at his feeble attempt at humor, thinking she'd always liked that side of him. Glancing at the brightly colored picture Savannah had been coloring, she reminded herself that she'd been over this before, too, and as beguiling as his humorous side was, it wasn't enough.

She walked to the windowsill where her spring flowers bloomed. Until she'd come to Jasper Gulch she'd been like those daffodils and crocuses and hyacinths whose roots were only as deep as the clear glass bottles that held them. She'd grown up in a dozen different towns in a dozen different states. None of them had felt like home, especially after her mother had died. Certainly, none of them drew her back. During the first years of her marriage to Nick she'd done everything in her power to turn their tiny apartment into a home. At first she'd thought the burglars who'd broken in had robbed her of her sense of tranquillity and the feeling that their four walls were a safe haven. As the months had passed, she'd realized that the burglars hadn't taken that. Somewhere along the way she and Nick had lost that sense of tranquillity on their own.

Here, in this big old house in Jasper Gulch, she'd found a piece of herself that had been missing for a long time. She didn't want to lose it again. She wished there was some way to make Nick understand.

She'd exchanged faded blue jeans for the skirt she'd been wearing that morning, but the white sweater was still the same. The sleeves were a little too long, but it was warm and comfortable. She curled her hands over the cuffs, then deftly crossed her arms. Trying to soften the words she had to say, she gave Nick a small smile. "We've both come a long way these past six months. I don't want to hurt you, Nick, but if we told people we're trying to reconcile, it *would* be a lie."

"That's not the way I see it."

"Isn't it? Savannah needs her father. She loves you, and God knows you love her, but let's not confuse the issue or lose sight of the real reason you're here. The thought of that little girl facing danger turns my stomach, but if she *has* to face it, I can't think of anybody I'd trust more than you to keep her safe."

Nick studied Brittany thoughtfully. There was something in the tone of her voice that sounded like accusation. It put him on edge and sharpened the tone of his own voice. "She's not the only person I intend to keep safe, dammit."

The spark of some indefinable emotion flickered in her eyes, only to die away as she said, "I know, Nick. I know." She glanced out the doorway to the living room where Savannah's voice rang with laughter. "It sounds as if the popcorn's ready. You'd better hurry if you want any. For someone so small, your daughter can really pack it away."

"Brittany, wait."

She turned in the doorway. Now that he had her attention, he didn't know what to say. She smiled, albeit sadly, then slowly left the room. Nick stayed where he was, trying to figure out what had brought that unspoken pain alive in her eyes. He couldn't shake the feeling that it was somehow his fault.

Hell, that was nothing new. He took complete responsibility for messing up Brittany's life. Whether she liked it or not he intended to take complete responsibility for keeping her and Savannah in one piece from now on.

He stared into the darkness outside the window, one hand on the wall on either side of the glass. A chilly wind rattled the shutters, but the ache in his chest wasn't from the cold. The pain was nearly as sharp as it had been the night Brittany had shown him the advertisement luring women to Jasper Gulch. He hadn't wanted to lose her, but six months ago he'd had no choice but to let them go. The knowledge that Brittany was taking back her maiden name had felt like a kick in the stomach, but that, too, had been out of his control.

And then he'd received that magazine article in the mail. He wasn't surprised Dawson had recognized Brittany in the magazine article. Her classic bone structure and dark hair and eyes were pretty damned unforgettable.

Letting her go hadn't kept her safe. Letting her go felt like the biggest mistake he'd ever made. And Nicholas Colter had made a helluva lot of them.

"Hurry, Daddy," Savannah called, "before Crystal and me eat all the popcorn ourself."

Nick pasted a smile on his face and walked into the next room.

"My, my," Mertyl said, rising feebly to her feet and pains-takingly switching off the television set in the corner. "If I were twenty years younger I'd send that Morley Safer a fan letter."

Morley Safer? Crystal mouthed to Brittany, placing the empty popcorn bowl on the coffee table in front of her.

Brittany gave her friend a bland smile and a noncommittal shrug. She couldn't help it. She was having a hard time concentrating.

Mertyl Gentry and her husband, Fred, had run the town's only grocery store for more than forty years. After Fred's death twelve years ago, Mertyl had operated the mom and pop business by herself. She was spry for an eighty-four-year-old, although recently minor health problems had begun to slow her down. Five months ago she'd sold the store and had moved into Brittany's boarding house, becoming her first paying boarder. Normally, Mertyl retired to her room about the same time Brittany put Savannah to bed, but tonight the old woman's favorite Sunday evening television program had been preempted by a sporting event and had aired a half hour later than usual. And Mertyl never missed "Sixty Minutes," no matter how late she had to stay up.

"Come along, Daisy," she called, making her way up the open staircase. "Good night, girls. You, too, young man."

Brittany and Crystal called good-night, but the only man in the room barely mumbled a reply. Nick had done a pretty good job of pretending to be even tempered while Savannah had been awake. In the half hour she'd been in bed he'd rattled every window latch and jiggled every doorknob and generally prowled the lower level of the house like a caged cougar.

Noisily licking salt and butter from the tips of her fingers, Crystal looked from Brittany to Nick. "Throwing an attractive man into a household of women is like throwing a chili pepper into a pot of borscht. Suddenly cold beet soup has a whole new flavor, doesn't it?"

"Cold beet soup?" Brittany asked.

"A chili pepper?" Nick asked at the same time.

Crystal raised both hands and steadily backed toward the stairs. "Think about it. Myrtle suddenly has a crush on the man on Sixty Minutes. I'm trying to remember how long it's been since I've so much as been on a date, and Brittany, you were so lost in your own daydreams you didn't even smile at my humor. Can you think of a better explanation for the sudden and complete change in group dynamics around here?"

Nick didn't miss the meaningful look of warning Brittany gave to her friend, but he thought better of mentioning it. Instead, he stared at the woman wearing the gauzy skirt and bangle bracelets and asked, "You seem to know an awful lot about group dynamics. Are you a psychologist, Crystal?"

Crystal's nod looked a lot like a shrug. "I have a little piece of paper that says I can be if I want to be."

"If you have a degree in psychology what are you doing here?"

Her smile was the tiniest bit shaky. "I'm practicing my people skills, what else? How am I doing so far? On second thought, don't answer that. I'll just mosey up to my room and leave you two alone to begin World War III."

She disappeared up the stairs with an agility and speed that belied the appearance she tried to project. Staring after her, Nick asked, "Did she happen to mention what planet she's from?"

Brittany lowered the cup of tea she'd been sipping. "Her past history is long and varied, but she's from earth, believe me."

Running a hand through his hair, Nick said, "I don't know anything about her philosophy on group dynamics, but she's wrong about World War III. I don't want to argue with you."

Brittany met his gaze with a steady look of her own. "I hope you don't expect me to ask what you'd rather do."

He released his breath all at once and felt a small smile crack his face. Striding to the big picture window, he said, "It's the wind. And this waiting. Both are driving me crazy."

Brittany slid to the edge of the cushion and deftly rose to her feet. Being careful to keep a safe distance between her and Nick, she said, "You might get used to the wind out here, but I doubt you'll ever be comfortable with waiting."

He continued to stare out the window. "I need something to do. If my father was here he'd point me toward a pile of logs that needed splitting."

Brittany smiled at the mention of Nick's father. She hadn't always agreed with Joe Colter's opinions, but she'd always liked him. Noting the set of Nick's shoulders and the stiffness of his back, she thought she could say the same for Joe's second son.

"This situation would wear on anyone's nerves, Nick. Do you think it's possible that this is all a hoax designed by Dawson to make you miserable and keep you looking over your shoulder for the rest of your life?"

Nick answered without turning around. "It's possible, but my instincts tell me it isn't likely."

Brittany studied his reflection in the dark window. "Are your instincts telling you he's nearby?"

When he shook his head she sighed in relief. "Then you're right. You do need something to do. About the only place that doesn't roll up its sidewalks at eight o'clock is the Crazy Horse Saloon."

"The Crazy Horse Saloon, huh? Are you trying to get rid of me, Brittany?"

He finally turned to face her, but she didn't answer, because in a way that's exactly what she was trying to do.

Nick slammed the gear shift into Park and climbed out of his car. He'd driven around town for a while, putting streets and visual markers to memory. Somehow, he'd ended up on the interstate, his foot pressed to the floor in an attempt to burn the carbon out of his exhaust system and the frustration out of the pit of his stomach. His car was purring like a pussycat. His stomach was still in knots. All because Brittany's answer to his earlier question had been written all over her face.

Oh, yes, she was most definitely trying to get rid of him.

He scowled as he pushed through the heavy door, taking in the interior of the Crazy Horse Saloon in one glance. The place wasn't exactly crawling with people. It looked as if the regulars liked it that way. Cletus McCully, the old man he'd talked to at the wedding reception the previous night, nodded from a table way in the back where he and three of his cronies were playing cards. A plump woman with bleached blond hair was wiping down the bar around a barrel-chested man who was perched on a stool beside her. The gray-haired man Nick had momentarily mistaken for Kipp Dawson paused in the story he was telling his buddies, one of whom was Forrest Wilkie, the rancher who'd nearly fallen down trying to kiss Brittany last night.

The knot in Nick's gut tightened.

The jukebox changed songs about the same time he dropped onto a bar stool and released a breath of pent-up air. Within seconds the bleached blonde had plunked a shot glass in front of him. "Sugar, you look like you could use a stiff drink and a willing woman. Not necessarily in that order."

Nick found himself staring into the eyes of a woman whose makeup didn't come close to hiding the lines in her face. If he was a betting man he'd say she'd seen her share of heartache and had moved on to happier times.

With a lift of her brows and a nod toward a tall brown bottle, she said, "The first shot is on the house."

Nicholas Colter rarely drank. It had nothing to do with religion or principle or anything as righteous as that. He didn't drink because alcohol dulled the senses, and a man in his profession tended to need his wits about him. He scowled all over again as he remembered the expression he'd seen on Brittany's face when she'd suggested he come here tonight. Shrugging, he pushed the glass toward the bartender. "Maybe just one."

She poured the shot of whiskey, then righted the bottle without spilling a drop. Nick stared at the amber-colored liquid and then at the plain gold wedding band on his left hand. Taking the glass between his thumb and middle finger, he knocked the shot back in one gulp.

"Feel any better?" the female bartender asked when he plunked the glass back to the counter.

Nick figured it would take the rest of the bottle to make him feel better, but he nodded, anyway.

"My name's DoraLee Brown. That good-lookin' cowboy at the other end of the bar is my new husband, Boomer. Want me to leave the bottle?"

Nick eyed DoraLee then her husband and then the bottle. "If I drink it here it'll only run out the holes those men are drilling into my back with their glares."

DoraLee's laugh was more like a cackle, but it seemed to remove the edge from the air. By the time another song started on the jukebox, the Sunday-night regulars had gone back to their poker and tall tales.

DoraLee leaned her elbows on the bar and winked one well-made-up eye. "Small-town people are notorious for their pre-occupation with strangers and gossip. The folks of Jasper Gulch are no exception. You can hardly blame them, now, can you? Half the people in town saw you and Brittany leave the weddin' reception last night, and the other half knew about it by morning. Anybody with a lick of sense could see that there are still sparks between you two, and most folks automatically assumed...well, you know."

Nick swallowed the sudden tightness in his throat, but there wasn't much he could do about the tightness taking up residence elsewhere in his body. He reached for a bowl of pretzels, not to eat, but to give him someplace else to focus.

"You don't feel like talking about it, huh, sugar?"

The negative sound Nick made earned him another cackle of laughter. "Then you're in luck, because all you've gotta do is listen. Now I'm not gonna get on my high horse. If you had known my first husband you'd understand why I'm not exactly an expert on marriage, but Boomer has taught me a thing or two about love since then, and I'd like to pass on a few words of advice to you. First you're gonna have to answer a few questions.''

Nick glanced at DoraLee and then at her husband at the other end of the bar. "Is she for real?" Nick's expression asked.

Boomer's shrug and subsequent nod pretty much said it all.

"I'm not going to judge, but I've gotta ask," DoraLee said, quietly drawing Nick's attention. "Have you done anything unforgivable?''

Another time Nick would have walked away. Something way in the back of DoraLee's eyes made him decide to stay. "Unforgivable?" he repeated quietly.

"Yes. You know. Did you beat her or fool around on her—that was my Delbert's downfall. He had an eye for the rodeo bunnies. That man broke my heart a hundred times. Did you do something to break Brittany's? Did you drink up your paycheck, or break any laws? Some folks can forgive those things, but it makes it a lot harder, and marriage is hard enough, ya know?''

Yeah. Nick knew. But he sat up straighter, and after a fair amount of deliberation he shook his head.

DoraLee beamed. "That's what I thought. In that case, I'm taking the liberty of continuing. Now, I don't know Brittany very well. She seems sweet, but other than startin' the Jasper Gulch Historic Society, she's pretty much kept to herself since moving here. Far as I know she only accepted a date from one man, and that was Clayt Carson, and they only had lunch. It's a good thing, because Mel McCully, Melody Carson, Clayt's wife now, might have scratched her eyes out if it had been anything more than that. But that's another story.''

Nick watched DoraLee closely, wishing she would stick to the topic at hand. "What are you saying?"

Grinning at herself, she said, "I'm saying a lot of things, aren't I? But I guess what I'm trying to say is this. I saw the way Brittany's eyes lit up when she first laid them on you last night, and I could practically feel the sparks fly between the two of you. Now, I'll be the first to admit that I held on to my first marriage too long. But a lot of folks give up too soon. The trick is finding the middle ground and deciding if there's anything left to hold on to. I guess that's what you have to decide.''

The old men in the back of the room called for another round. Casting Nick a wink, DoraLee grasped four long-neck bottles in her hands and sashayed out from behind the bar. Her husband smiled at her as she passed by. She smiled lovingly in return. Something inside Nick went very still. Brittany used to smile at *him* like that. There wasn't much he wouldn't do to have her look at him that way again.

He turned a pretzel over and over in his hand, thinking about some of the things DoraLee had said. Had he given up too soon? And what on God's green earth could he do about it if he had?

Nick didn't have all the answers when he pulled to a stop in front of the boarding house at the stroke of midnight, but he knew where he had to start. He paused at the locked door. After checking under the doormat for a spare key, he took a wire from his pocket and picked the lock for the second time that day.

He would take care of that little problem first thing in the morning. Right now there was something else he had to do.

He closed the door and quietly locked it before switching off the porch light. Someone had left a lamp on for him in the living room, but Brittany was nowhere in sight. Listening intently, he shrugged out of his coat, quietly making his way toward the short hall that led to the two bedrooms on the main floor. He paused in Savannah's doorway. She was sleeping peacefully, one hand tucked beneath her chin, a pale blue night-light casting the room in soft illumination. She'd started needing a night-light after the break-in two years ago. Maybe his little girl hadn't quite fully recovered from that trauma, after all. A knot solidified in his throat, leaving a bad taste in his mouth and a worse feeling in the pit of his stomach.

Reminding himself that she was doing a lot better these days, he made his way to the next door. It wasn't latched and required only the slightest push to open it all the way. He stayed where he was for a moment, uncertain what to do next.

Brittany was sleeping.

She was covered to her waist, pillows propped behind her, a book opened on her chest. She'd never been able to read in bed. That might have been because he'd always thought of more interesting things to do there. He drew in a deep breath and forbade himself to continue thinking in that vein. Still, he remained frozen in indecision. Before he'd decided whether to call her name or wait until morning, she opened her eyes.

"Did I wake you?" he asked.

"Was I sleeping?"

Nick smiled to himself. Brittany had always answered his questions with a question of her own. It used to irritate the bejiggers out of him. It was amazing how much he'd missed it.

Her eyes looked dark and deep, her hair slightly mussed. She was wearing a white knit shirt, its sleeves long, a tiny rosebud button at her throat. The book was lying across her breasts. He wondered what she would do if she knew how badly he wanted to push it out of the way, to toss it to the floor and glide his hands in its place.

Allowing himself to take only three steps, he said, "What are you reading?"

She wet her lips and swallowed nervously. "It's a book about Deadwood and Wild Bill Hickok and the gold rush in the Black Hills."

Of course. She was reading about history. Of their own volition, his eyes roamed her features. She looked the same as she always had, and yet different. "You're hair's longer."

Her hand went to her hair and then to her throat. Nick

couldn't help noticing that she was still wearing her wedding ring. Slowly she gestured to the hall. "I locked all the doors. Just in case...well, you know. I was trying to wait up for you so I could unlock it."

Nick nodded. "I let myself in. God, you're beautiful."

Their eyes met, held. She was the first to look away. "So you made it to the Crazy Horse."

"How can you tell?"

"You smell like Cletus McCully's cigars."

Nick's laughter sounded rusty to his own ears. Strangely, it felt good. "I played a game of poker with him. He cheats."

"I've heard that." Her eyes held him where he was. "Have you been drinking?" she whispered.

"Mostly I've been thinking. About you. And me."

"I don't think that's very wise, Nick."

He shrugged. Nobody had ever accused him of being wise. "An interesting place, the Crazy Horse. I talked to DoraLee and Boomer Brown. Forrest Wilkie shot invisible daggers at me most of the night. I wanted to tell him he doesn't stand a chance with you. Not because he isn't a decent enough man, but because you and I are going to try again."

She pushed herself up on her elbows and held up one hand. He doubted she intended him to take it, but he twined his fingers around hers and leaned closer. "I didn't tell him that. Partly out of deference to you, and partly because I know how it feels to want you and not be able to have you. That's what I came in here to tell you."

"Nick."

"I gave up too easily before. Kipp Dawson's threat may have been what brought me to Jasper Gulch, but I intend to show you that I've changed. I want to try again. Just one more chance. That's all I'm asking for."

She opened her mouth to speak again.

"Don't say it. Don't say we've already tried a hundred times. I didn't come in here to argue. I came in for only one thing." His gaze dropped to her mouth. "Or maybe two."

His mouth covered hers in the middle of her gasp. Her lips were soft and warm and so damn sweet he couldn't think. Some thread of good sense kept him from stretching out on the bed beside her and pressing his body next to hers and touching her in all the places that would turn her pliant and willing in his arms. He knew that wouldn't be fair.

Of all times for his conscience to surface.

He also knew that if he wanted to win her back, he was going to have to mind his p's and q's. He was going to have to show her that he'd changed and that their marriage was worth fighting for.

Much, much too soon, the kiss ended. They opened their eyes, swallowed. He was the first to find his voice. "Good night, Brittany."

She opened her mouth, only to clamp it shut again. He'd surprised her. It was amazing how much he liked the feeling.

"I don't know what to say," she whispered.

"Say good night."

Her eyes softened, a smile pulling at her mouth. "Sleep well, Nick."

A growl erupted from his throat. "I don't expect to be able to sleep at all, not after that kiss. Do you have any suggestions?"

"One comes to mind."

Nick groaned. Long before his hormones had finished arguing with his conscience, she was shaking her head. "It's not what you're thinking."

"How do you know what I'm thinking?"

She let her gaze trail down his body. By the time she made it back to his face her eyebrows were arched knowingly. "If I were a doctor, I'd tell you to take two aspirin and call me in the morning."

"A doctor would know better."

"And so do we."

He stared at her for a long time. Finally he said, "You're right. We can discuss this further in the morning. I can hardly wait." He glanced over his shoulder in the doorway. "Where did you say you keep the aspirin?"

He was gone an instant later. She couldn't remember the last time they'd parted with a smile.

She turned out the light. Lying in the dark, she listened for the sound of Nick's footsteps. She heard him pause briefly at Savannah's door. Moments later his shoes sounded on the stairs.

She closed the book she'd been reading and placed it on the nightstand. Punching her pillow down, she pressed her cheek into its softness and snuggled under the warm blankets. When she'd first awakened and found Nick looking at her she'd thought she'd been dreaming. Smoothing her fingertips over her lips, she took a deep breath. That kiss might have had all the qualities of a sweet dream, but the scent of cigar smoke hanging in the air was real.

Nick had come in after working late and made many midnight *appearances* in bed in the past, but this was the first time he'd left after only one kiss. She thought about everything he'd said tonight and a few of the things he'd only insinuated with the tilt of his head or his rusty half smiles. He said he'd changed. Maybe he had. The old Nick never would have kissed her as if he'd go crazy if he couldn't have her, then let it go at that. The old Nick would have stoked the passion between them until they'd both been overcome with raw need. The old Nick wouldn't have told her they would talk about it in the morning. He wouldn't have wanted to talk at all.

The man she'd married nearly seven years ago had been consumed with responsibility and guilt. Was it possible that he felt more for her than a sense of obligation and duty?

Airy hopes filled her mind and her chest. Was Nick right? Had they given up too soon? Should they try one more time?

Did she dare to hope?

She closed her eyes and took a deep breath, thinking that if hope had a scent, it would be the smell of cigar smoke lingering in her room. If it had a texture, it would be the smoothness of Nick's lips. If hope had only one image, it would be his barely there smile.

The old Nick had rarely smiled.

Had he changed?

Impossible, her better judgment insisted.

Not so, whispered through her mind. Wasn't anything possible with enough love? Perhaps they would both know the answer in the morning.

Chapter Five

Brittany awoke to sunlight streaming through her window and the smell of coffee—strong coffee. The kind of strong coffee Nick used to make.

She squinted against the sunshine, trying to open her eyes. Wait a minute. The sun was shining? The sun had to be up in order to be shining.

She was halfway across the room before she took her next breath. It was after eight. She never set an alarm clock. With Savannah she'd never needed one. Brittany came to a screeching halt in her daughter's room. Savannah's bed was empty, her closet door ajar. Brittany raced toward the kitchen where she came to a halt all over again.

She pushed her hair out of her eyes and tried to dispel the grogginess that came from sleeping too long. Savannah, on the other hand, looked as if she'd been up for hours. She was dressed in a red turtleneck shirt, a calico print vest and matching ruffled skirt. She was even wearing red tights and a red bow in her hair. All smiles, she turned around at the table.

"Hi, Mommy!"

"Savannah, why didn't you wake me?"

"Daddy was sleeping on the couch again, so I woke him up. We've been real quiet, haven't we, Daddy?"

Nick walked into the room from the other direction, his husky morning voice drawing her gaze. "We both agreed to treat you to a little rest. *Do* you feel more rested this morning, Brittany?"

He'd stopped near the sink looking for all the world as sleep rumpled as he sounded. His shirt was wrinkled, his jeans faded, his shoelaces untied. She knew from experience that the sleepy look of his eyes was deceiving and could turn calculating and alert at the slightest hint of a crisis.

"Did you help Savannah get ready for school?" she asked.

He nodded. "Did you sleep well?"

"Mmm-hmm." Her eyes went out of focus somewhere around his shoulders. "Did you?"

By the time her gaze made it back to his face it was too late to call back her words. He was looking at her with a lift of his eyebrows and a twist of his lips that could only mean trouble. Stretching his hands over his head, he said, "Actually, I had a little trouble falling asleep. The aspirin didn't help."

Emotions stirred inside Brittany, dropping from her neck to her chest to her stomach like a curtain unfolding on a stage. She knew what the sensation meant. Part of it was desire in its purest form. She was old enough to control her desire. The problem was what she felt for Nick had always been more than desire. She loved him, and she'd never known how to control that.

"Do you have a headache, Daddy?" Savannah asked, licking something sticky from her finger.

Brittany and Nick both glanced down at their daughter and then at each other. Nick smiled, his grin slowly giving way to laughter. "That feels good," he said, before squatting down to tie his shoes. "No, I don't have a headache. In fact, I feel better than I've felt in a long, long time."

The meaning behind his words went over Savannah's head, but it hit Brittany right between the eyes. The truth was she hadn't felt this way in a long time, either. She could have blamed it on the sunshine, but she knew there was more to it than that.

"Aren't you glad Daddy came for a visit, Mommy?"

Both Nick and Savannah were looking at her, waiting for her answer. Brittany couldn't manage more than a small smile. She *was* glad for Savannah's sake, but the feelings Nick was slowly awakening inside *her* left her feeling uncertain, shaky. When she'd first moved to Jasper Gulch she'd felt sad, of course. But she'd done it with a sense of purpose and the conviction that she was putting the past behind her and moving forward with her life. Nick's arrival in Jasper Gulch made that forward motion feel more like a circle. Last night she'd thought anything was possible. This morning she reminded herself that she'd thought that dozens of times before.

Savannah reached for her glass of milk. It slipped out of her hands before she took the last swallow. The glass shattered on the floor, but it was Savannah's screech that sent both Nick and Brittany into action. "It's all right," she crooned in her daughter's ear. "It's just milk."

"That's right," Nick declared, lifting Savannah away from the jagged pieces of glass. "And everyone knows there's no sense crying over spilled milk."

Carefully picking up shards of glass, Brittany thought about what Nick had said. Cletus McCully had said something similar a few weeks ago, only he'd been referring to her divorce. Wiping up the liquid that had splattered in every direction on the worn linoleum, Brittany thought that spoiled marriages had very little in common with spilled milk, because she'd cried plenty after leaving Nick. She'd promised herself she was done crying. And she'd thought Savannah was beyond going to pieces over an accidentally broken glass.

"There, Savannah," Brittany said the moment she was finished. "See? The floor's as good as new."

For a moment the expression in her little girl's eyes broke Brittany's heart. Savannah stood next to Nick, her small hand clasped in his, her face wet from tears. It was an expression she'd worn much of the time before they'd moved here. Sighing, she climbed onto her father's knee. "Daddy fixed pancakes for breakfast. Homemade."

Brittany glanced at the spilled flour, the cracked eggs and dribbled batter on the counter directly behind Nick. He'd never been one of those men who insisted a woman's place was in the kitchen. He'd always enjoyed puttering around there. But, Lord, what a mess.

"If you hurry," he said, rising to his feet slowly, "you'll have enough time to get dressed and come with me while I drop Savannah off at school. After that I want to pick up a few things in Pierre. We could talk on the way."

Glancing at the clock on the stove, she shook her head. "If you'd like to take Savannah to school, it would be a big help this morning, but Mertyl will be wanting her oatmeal at nine. Crystal usually comes home for lunch, and I'm expecting two new boarders any day, which means I have a lot of work to do to get their rooms ready."

"Were you planning to squeeze me into your schedule, Brittany?"

She mulled over his question while helping Savannah into her coat and hat. Giving the child a hug goodbye, Brittany felt Nick's eyes on her. Meeting his gaze, she nodded. "We can talk when you get back if you'd like."

He reached for Savannah's hand and gave Brittany a look that said he'd be back. The determination in his eyes dallied around the edges of her mind while she stood in the middle of her cluttered kitchen after he and Savannah had gone.

Taking a mug from the cupboard, she poured herself a cup of steaming coffee. She took one sip, sputtered and promptly turned on the burner beneath the teakettle. Nick's coffee was the reason she'd developed a taste for tea.

Their tastes clashed on scores of other things, as well. She craved chocolate; he didn't even like sweets. She loved to talk; talking made him uncomfortable. She liked brown rice and steamed vegetables; rare steak was his diet's mainstay. They *did* have a few things in common. Their mutual love for Savannah was one of them. They both believed in the powers that be, and they both wanted goodness to prevail over evil. And they shared an attraction that defied reason and overrode resentment. It felt incredible and very dangerous. They also happened to share a mutual dislike for arguments of any kind. And yet they'd argued about practically everything under the sun.

How in the world had their relationship gotten so completely out of control? Was Nick right? Was it possible that they'd given up too soon? Savannah was happy here. Could Nick ever feel the same?

Glancing around the room, she knew she had a lot of thinking to do. And a lot of work ahead of her. Maybe the answer would come to her. Or maybe it was deep inside Nick, and she would never know for sure.

Brittany paused to catch her breath in the middle of the living room. The kitchen was spotless, her shower but a memory. She'd made beds, shaken rugs and cracked a window in the two bedrooms she was preparing for her new boarders. There was dusting to do, her account book to balance, a load of freshly dried towels to fold, but except for Nick's faded T-shirt lying on the floor, the house was in order.

She scooped up the shirt and slowly brought it to her face. Nick must have taken a shower after he went upstairs last night. He never wore aftershave or cologne. She thought the clean scent of soap and man clinging to his shirt was better than anything that could have come out of a bottle. Since she couldn't very well stand around absorbing his scent all day, she folded the clean shirt over her arm and headed for the stairs where she'd left a bucket of cleaning products.

She deposited everything except the shirt in the room at the end of the hall before making a bee-line for Nick's room. The door was ajar. Other than the rumpled appearance of the bed, the room showed no signs of being lived in. She paused, uncertain what to do. Technically Nick was still her husband. Still, they'd been separated for six months. This was his room, and she wasn't sure she had a right to be here.

Deciding it wouldn't hurt to simply take care of the shirt, she strolled around the double bed and opened the closet door. A battered suitcase with a broken clasp and an overstuffed duffel bag were heaped on the floor. Otherwise the closet was empty.

She was in the process of placing the shirt on a high shelf when her hand nicked the corner of a small box. The box teetered on its edge, tipped forward and toppled into the air. Brittany caught it in midair before it hit the floor.

Her fingers shook as she lifted the flap. Nestled inside were dozens of brass-colored bullets. She took a few into her hand, thinking about what they were used for, about the pain they caused and the people they protected.

"It looks like I've finally got you right where I want you."

She spun around, her heart in her throat. "Nick, you scared me."

The man had an uncanny ability to move without making a sound. It was disconcerting. His mother once told Brittany she'd put bells on both her sons' shoes when they were small so she would know where they were. There were probably a lot of criminals who wouldn't have minded using similar tactics on the Colter brothers today.

The way Nick was leaning in the doorway made her wonder how long he'd been there. He pushed himself to an upright position, but he didn't stroll any closer. "There's no need to be afraid of me, Brittany. I'm just a man."

She drew in one shaky breath and then another. Her heart had dislodged itself from her throat and was beating a steady rhythm in her chest. It was a response she'd become accustomed to a long time ago. She closed her hand, torn between a wish that things could be different and the cold metal cartridges pressing into her palm.

Nick's jeans were slung low on his hips, his cheeks slightly ruddy from the wind, his eyes a deep shade of blue. No matter what he said, he wasn't *just* a man. He was a cop who did what it took to put bad people behind bars. Savannah was thrilled with her father's visit, but the slight ridge under the left side of his coat was proof that he wasn't like the other fathers in town. They didn't carry guns.

He ambled into the room, eyeing the box in her hand. "I put them on the highest shelf, out of harm's way."

"Oh. I mean, that's good. I wasn't really snooping."

"I didn't say you were." Nick didn't know why she was having so much trouble meeting his eyes.

"I found your shirt downstairs, that's all, and I was taking care of it."

"Brittany, it's all right. I don't mind. I don't have anything to hide."

She looked up at him, her eyes wide and wary, her lips parted as if she wanted to ask him something. "What is it?" He touched her shoulder, gently gliding his hand down her arm. He'd intended his touch to be a companionable gesture. Companionable, hell. The merest brush of his palm on the smooth fabric covering her skin sent need shooting up his arm.

She shook her head, peering at him through dark brown strands of hair that reached almost to her eyelashes. A lump came and went in his throat. He ached to brush those strands away from her forehead, to bury his hands in the wispy tresses behind her ears and slowly draw her closer. Something in her eyes held him still.

She wet her lips and quietly said, "I noticed you haven't unpacked your things."

"I'm better at making messes than making myself at home. Besides, I was hoping you'd invite me to *unpack* in your room."

Brittany gasped. She tried to swallow, but it didn't help. He'd sideswiped her, plain and simple.

"Are you thinking about it?" he asked, his hand gliding

farther down her arm. "If you're not, you'd better tell me, because standing this close to you is really getting my hopes up."

She shook her head and fought a grin. The man had no rules when it came to double meanings. "You're incorrigible."

"I know."

His presence was working its magic on her; his deep, husky voice dissolving her misgivings one by one. She dumped the bullets into the box and deposited the small case back on the shelf where it belonged. Tilting her head thoughtfully, she said, "You and Cletus McCully share similar scruples."

It was his turn to open his mouth only to clamp it shut and try again. "If you're trying to make me humble, it's working. Please tell me you don't believe I'm anything like that crotchety old man."

"You don't think Cletus is sweet?"

"You think I'm sweet?"

She crossed her arms and shook her head to clear it. This bantering was making her dizzy, yet she was amazed at how much she was enjoying it. In an effort to get back on an even footing, she said, "You said you wanted to talk this morning."

He stared at her for what seemed like forever before finally nodding. "I do, but first I have to level with you. I've been invited to the spring dance by the second prettiest girl in town."

Brittany felt herself melting a little more. "Is that a fact?"

He nodded. "Are you jealous?"

Her smile was the only indication that she was on to him. "That depends. Is this girl about yea tall, have a sweet disposition, eyes the exact color of her father's and an internal alarm clock that's set to go off before the sun comes up?"

"So you think I'm sweet *and* you like the color of my eyes?"

"Sometimes I think you're sweet. Other times I think you're impossible."

"Which would you say I am right now?"

Brittany didn't know what was taking place in her mind, but she knew what was happening elsewhere in her body. Emotions stirred within her. She felt herself slipping into the blue of his eyes, falling into his barely there smile, losing herself in him an inch at a time. She'd felt this way before, dozens of times, but she couldn't allow it to happen again. At least not until she found the courage to ask him the one question she'd never been able to voice before.

Taking a backward step, she said, "Nick, if we're ever going to be able to make sense of what's happening between us, we have to set up a few ground rules."

"Ground rules?"

"Number one. Ex-husbands can't ask questions ex-wives can't answer."

"I never wanted the divorce, Brittany. And I'm not your ex-husband."

"You will be in less than two weeks."

"It would only take one word from you to change that."

Brittany closed her eyes. No, she thought. It would only take one word from him. One word that meant everything. One word he'd tripped over a few times when they were first married but hadn't uttered since. One word that described an emotion she was afraid he'd never truly felt for her. Love. Had he ever loved her? Or had he only married her because Savannah was on the way?

The furnace rumbled on, warm air streaming through the register in the floor. Otherwise, the house was quiet. Nick glanced at the patch of hallway visible through the open door. "Are we alone, Brittany?"

"For now. Mertyl hasn't quite gotten used to being retired. She spends most mornings at the grocery store helping the new owners. I pick Savannah up from kindergarten at twelve-thirty. Crystal works part of the day for Doc Masey and the other part for Luke Carson's vet service. She's been known to lend a helping hand down at Melody Carson's diner, too.''

Nick noticed the flicker of happiness way in the back of Brittany's eyes. She seemed in her element here. He knew she was a mature woman, capable of raising their child and running her boarding house, and yet for a moment she seemed more like the young girl he'd met ten years ago. He didn't know the exact date the light had left her eyes. He only knew he didn't want history to repeat itself. He didn't want to wake up tomorrow and see dullness where her sunshine had been, to hear sadness where there had been laughter.

Maybe she was right. Maybe they did need to lay a few ground rules. Perhaps then he could lure those warm smiles out of her and convince her that they belonged together.

Dropping his hands into his coat pockets, he said, ''Did you say Crystal works for a Carson?''

''Luke Carson, the area veterinarian. Why?''

''That name sure comes up a lot. Two nights ago you told me it was a Carson who founded this town. Last night DoraLee mentioned that someone named Carson snagged the first woman who moved here last summer. The woman who owns the diner is married to another one. There's a Carson spread a few miles west of town. How many Carsons are there, anyway?''

Brittany had turned her attention to the rumpled bedspread. Smoothing out the worst of the wrinkles, she said, ''You make it sound as if there are dozens of them, but there are only three Carson men. Luke and Clayt and their father, Hugh.''

''Which one did you go out with?''

Her hand stilled on Nick's pillow. ''How did you know I went out with one of them?''

He strode around to the other side of the bed and pulled up the blankets on that side. ''Small-town people are notorious for their preoccupation with newcomers and gossip. DoraLee said so herself. She also mentioned that you went out with a man by the name of Carson. Why, was it supposed to be a secret?''

She straightened as if she needed a moment to reorient herself. ''Of course not,'' she sputtered. ''It's just that it isn't true. I mean, I had lunch with Clayt one day, but it wasn't a date. I haven't dated anybody since—''

''Since me?''

He watched her throat convulse on a swallow. After a time she shook her head. Nick had another uncustomary urge to grin. ''In that case, how about having lunch with me?''

''Now?''

''Unless you can think of something else you'd rather do.''

They both glanced at the bed between them. ''No,'' she said, taking a backward step toward the door. ''I think having lunch sounds like a good idea, a wise and timely and much-less-dangerous idea.''

Nick liked the expression on her face at that moment, her cheeks flushed, her eyes sparkling, but that wasn't all he liked. He liked the husky sound of her voice and the way his thoughts disintegrated and his breathing slowed. He liked the way his blood pounded through his body, rolling and pulsing its way into the part of him he was having a difficult time concealing. That wasn't all he liked, either. He liked the way she'd looked at him moments ago, as if she thought he was something pretty damn special. He liked that the best of all. In fact, in that instant he believed he could live without sex for the rest of his life as long as he could have this.

He glanced over his shoulder at his empty bed, then out the window toward the sky, hoping that lightning didn't strike him for having such a thought when he was consumed with so much need.

''Nick?''

Doing nothing to try to hide the throaty tremor in his voice, he said, ''If it's lunch you're wanting, we'd better get out of here.''

''Yes, of course. I'll get my coat.''

He moved toward her, thinking that was very prudent of her. But he called her a spoilsport just to see her smile.

Mel's Diner was on the east side of Main Street between the Jasper Gulch Clothing Store and the gas station on the corner. Its awning had probably been red a long time ago. Now it had faded to a color that had no name. Nick had been hoping the place would be all but deserted at 11:10 on a Monday morning, thereby giving him and Brittany a little privacy while awarding them the anonymity of a public place.

There was no such thing as anonymity in Jasper Gulch.

Six of the tables and two of the booths were occupied. He could only assume it had something to do with the food. It certainly wasn't due to the diner's decor. The place was as old and drab on the inside as it was on the outside. It was clean, though, and he must have been right about the food because the aromas wafting from the kitchen were mouth watering.

They seated themselves at a table in the center of the room. Nick had categorized every person in the diner seconds after entering. For someone DoraLee claimed had kept to herself since moving here, Brittany seemed to know everybody present on a first-name basis. She called hello, nodding and smiling and agreeing with someone named Rita, who was sitting in one of the booths, that spring was definitely in the air.

Keeping his eyes trained on the small menu and his voice low, Nick said, "You know what they're all thinking, don't you?"

Brittany studied Nick's face feature by feature. She knew what *he* was thinking. His chin was in his hand, his eyes seemingly trained on the menu. He might have been trying for an innocent look, but whenever his thoughts took a trip to the bedroom, the huskiness in his voice gave him away.

Strumming her fingers on the table, she finally said, "Something tells me it's going to be interesting to hear what you *think* they're thinking."

She could tell by the glint in his eyes that he was enjoying this as much as she was. "They're thinking here we are, two married people, living in the same house, having lunch together, smiling. They're putting two and two together, and Forrest Wilkie at least, doesn't like the answer he's coming up with."

Brittany glanced to the right where Forrest and his father were having an early lunch. Forrest did look a little forlorn. Leaning ahead slightly, she whispered, "If Forrest is down in the dumps, there's another reason. These people have a grapevine that's more accurate than the telegraph ever was. Mrs. Ferguson, the old woman who lives across the street from me, is sitting at the table by the window with Opal Graham and Isabell Pruitt. I'm sure she's told everyone that you're staying in the center bedroom at the top of the stairs."

He lowered his menu. "Then my reputation's ruined."

Brittany's sudden bout of laughter drew the gaze of every person in the room. Lowering her voice, she said, "Your reputation isn't ruined. These people might gossip, but they make up their own minds. The only way you're going to be able to win them over is by actions and deeds."

"And what will it take to win you over?"

She looked into his eyes, and couldn't turn away. *You already are,* she thought to herself. Every time he looked at her just so, every time he almost smiled, every time he lowered his voice to that husky baritone, he won her over a little more.

She swallowed, finally managing to pull herself together. Glancing at her hands, she said, "If you don't stop looking at me as if you'd rather have me for lunch than anything on that menu, I'm going to have to ask the good sheriff over there to arrest you."

Nick's gaze unerringly picked out of the crowd the man wearing the white cowboy hat and shiny badge. In his mid-thirties, the man had sandy-blond hair and wore a simple gold band on his left hand. He was broad-shouldered and lean, yet something about him made Nick think the man spent a good part of his time helping little old ladies cross the street.

"So that's the law in this town."

She nodded. "In this county. That's Cletus McCully's grandson, Wyatt. It might be a good idea to inform him of the reason you're in town."

Nick let his gaze drop from her eyes to her throat to the swell of her breasts covered by her navy sweater. "You think I should tell Sheriff McCully the reason I'm here?"

She crossed her arms in front of her and leaned her elbows on the table. "I meant the other reason. And you're doing it again, Nick."

He didn't apologize, because he wasn't sorry, but he put the menu down and cast another glance at the sheriff of Jones County. "I don't see how a sheriff from out here would be much help."

Brittany sighed. That meant Nick was going to try to take care of this situation by himself. "Have you heard from Dawson?" she asked. "Do you have any news of his whereabouts?"

Nick shook his head. "I called the station from a pay phone in Pierre this morning. Jake was on an assignment, but Pete was there. He said that my brother has been waiting for me to call. It seems there've been rumors that people have sighted Dawson, but nothing's been verified. I'm afraid all we can do is wait."

"Is everything all right over here?"

Nick's and Brittany's gazes both swung to the plump, gray-haired woman standing next to their table. Since Nick was a lot better at disguising his surprise, Brittany was the only one who jumped. "Oh," she exclaimed, "I didn't see you there."

"Of course you didn't," the kindly lady exclaimed. "Why, your eyes were so round you could have been discussing an ax murderer. I just came over to make sure you're not in some kind of trouble."

Brittany coughed, her eyes darting to Nick's.

"Opal, isn't it?" he asked, coming to her rescue.

"Why, yes, yes, it is." The older woman patted her bun

and literally preened. "I'm a little surprised you remembered my name."

"You shouldn't be surprised. Opal's a beautiful name."

Suddenly, Brittany understood where Louetta had acquired her tendency to blush. Opal's cheeks bore a faint pink hue just as her daughter's did much of the time.

"Tell me, Opal," Nick was saying, "have you had any leads as to the identity of the person or persons responsible for spiking that punch?"

While Opal rattled off the few things they'd discovered about the spiked punch incident, Brittany studied Nick in action. He nodded once or twice, asked a pointed question or two, and generally charmed the woman down to the roots of her gray hair.

After Opal left to amble back to her table beneath the window, Nick turned his attention back to Brittany. "What?" he asked after his first glimpse of her knowing expression.

Pressing her fingers over a crease in a paper napkin, she tilted her head and studied him thoughtfully. "It's nothing, really. I was just thinking that people would pay you a fortune to teach them how to do that."

"How to do what?"

"You turned Opal's attention away from her mention of an ax murderer with so much subtlety she won't realize you were hedging until next week."

"It's what I'm trained to do."

Brittany didn't argue, but there was more to Nick's ability than training. His intuition was uncanny and unexplainable. On a gut level, he seemed to know what to say and what not to say. It made him very interesting, and very difficult to know.

"Brittany?" He had leaned ahead in his chair. His eyes caught and held hers. "Now who's looking at who as if lunch is the last thing on her mind?"

The place surrounding Brittany's heart turned warm. It was as if a part of her she'd thought had died was slowly coming back to life. She wasn't sure she wanted it to come alive, but she didn't want to stop it, either. Nick had turned the tables on her, and she liked it. She'd forgotten how much fun sparring with him could be.

He blinked slowly and swallowed loudly. "What do you say we forget lunch?"

She swallowed, too, the action drawing his gaze to her mouth. The room turned hazy, and the noise faded away, until there was only him and her and this cloud of awareness surrounding them.

"I hate to interrupt, but would you two like to order?"

This time neither Brittany nor Nick jumped. They both glanced up at a slender, blond-haired woman wielding a coffee carafe. Brittany found herself responding to the knowing glint in Melody Carson's eyes. Placing both hands on the table, she said, "I, for one, would like the Monday special."

"I'll bet you would," the waitress said with a wink.

Brittany and Nick both glanced sideways in surprise but Nick was the first to laugh. "Make that two specials, will you?"

Nodding, Melody extended her right hand toward Nick. "I'm Melody Carson, the owner of this fine establishment."

"I'm—"

"Nick Colter. I heard."

Eyes narrowed, Nick studied Melody Carson. She was painfully blunt, blatantly forward and obviously very intuitive. She was also about six months pregnant. Resting her hand on her protruding stomach, she said, "Junior and I'll have your lunches to you in a few minutes."

Watching her walk away, Nick thought she was probably older than her freckles indicated. When she placed a hand on her lower back and refilled the sheriff's cup, Nick was reminded of how Brittany had looked when she'd been carrying Savannah. "How long have Melody and her husband been married?"

Brittany didn't fully understand the expression deep in

Nick's eyes, but she didn't like it. Keeping her chin level and her voice neutral, she said, "Not long." As an afterthought, she added, "They didn't have to get married, if that's what you're asking."

He clamped his mouth shut, the expression she'd glimpsed in his eyes moments ago rising to the surface again. They changed the subject, but something far more elemental had changed in the atmosphere in the small diner. Staring at Nick, Brittany knew that their attraction wasn't the only thing that was still alive between them.

They ate their chicken sandwiches and steaming potato chowder in relative silence. The sheriff pulled at the brim of his hat as they walked by to pay for their meal. Opal Graham's voice stopped them at the door. "Are you bringing Nicholas to the historic society meeting tomorrow night, Brittany?"

Pasting a smile on her face, she said, "We'll see, Opal."

Nick fiddled with the radio during the short drive back to the boarding house. Brittany could have told him there was no use trying to find another station. Out here every radio station played country-western music. But she let him figure it out for himself. It gave him something to do with his hands and gave her time to think.

He pulled the car into her driveway. When he cut the engine, she faced him and opened her mouth to speak. He kissed her before she'd uttered a sound. Her eyes widened in surprise then closed as if they had a will of their own. Nick had moved fast, but she still should have seen the kiss coming. It sent the pit of her stomach into a wild swirl and confused her even more.

Raising his face from hers, he whispered, "We never quite got around to setting up those ground rules. All I'm asking for is a chance to show you that I've changed."

She got out of the car without waiting for him, and was reaching for the Gone to lunch. Be back at twelve sign she'd left on the door when he caught up with her. Taking the key in hand, she started to unlock the door.

"Wait."

Nick's curt command froze her in place. Everything about him had gone on red alert. He was staring at a car parked down the street. His hands were in his coat pockets, his eyes were narrowed, his lips pressed in a straight line.

"What is it?" she whispered.

"I don't know. Maybe nothing. But that Cadillac has an Illinois license plate."

"Dawson's?"

He tested the knob on the front door. It was locked tight. He shrugged. "I don't know. Follow me."

Nick cast a practiced look up and down the street, automatically searching for possible hiding places. Hell, every place was a potential hiding place—every porch, every old shed, every shadow.

He slunk around two sides of the house, testing the locks on two more doors. Peering around one corner, he saw something move on the stoop off the doctor's study. A scraggly bush blocked his view, but he could make out the sides of two heads peering into the window. One person had brown hair. There was less of the other person visible, but the sun was definitely glinting off shaggy gray hair.

"What is it?" Brittany whispered behind him.

Nick shook his head without taking his eyes off that head. "Dawson?" she asked.

Nick felt for his gun. "Stay here. I'm going to find out."

He sprinted around the house, dodging the soggiest patches of lawn that might give away his presence by the sound. Unwilling to make the same mistake he'd made with Burke Kincaid, he kept his right hand underneath his jacket and stepped into view.

"Hold it right there."

The two figures swung around as Nick's fingers tightened around his gun.

Chapter Six

The wind whistling around the corner of the house blew through Nick's hair and plastered his coat to his back. His partner would have called his stance passive-aggressive. His feet appeared to be planted firmly on the ground, but if he so much as smelled something he didn't like or glimpsed somebody making one false move he would dive into action.

The adrenaline pumping through his body enabled him to see things more clearly, more quickly. Adrenaline or no adrenaline, he could hardly believe his eyes.

The strangely clad figures who had been peering through the windows stared at him and slowly put their hands in the air. "Is this a stick-up?" one called.

"My, he's a handsome one, isn't he?" the other said at the same time.

Nick pried his fingers from the butt of his gun and lowered his hand to his side. He wasn't ready to say that neither of them was a threat to society, but he knew without a doubt that they weren't a threat to Brittany or Savannah. They sure as hell weren't Dawson. For one thing, they were women. They might have been eccentric and they were definitely heading down the other side of the hill called middle age, but they were women none the less. Not that he'd never come up against a woman who would sooner take a chunk out of his hide than look at him. These two didn't seem to mind looking at him at all. In fact, one of them was ogling him as if he were a generous portion of peach pie à la mode.

"Sorry," he said with a grimace. "I thought you were someone else."

"Rats," the shorter of the two grumbled. "I was hoping you'd frisk us."

"Gussie!"

Batting fake eyelashes, the one named Gussie said, "Well I was. Are you one of the cowboys who advertised for women?"

Nick shook his head and held up both hands. He could face hardened criminals without flinching, but something about these two women gave him the urge to turn tail and run. From the looks of the rubies flashing on their chubby fingers, they were rich. Obviously they had no qualms about wearing real fur. A mink stole was wrapped around the taller woman's neck. And—

He took a couple of steps closer. "Is that a coonskin cap?" he asked the one called Gussie.

She dragged it off her head and smoothed her hand over the tail. "Well, um, yes. Yes, it is."

"I told you that folks out here don't wear such monstrosities anymore," the other woman admonished.

Brittany stepped out into the open. She'd heard the entire exchange, but she'd seldom seen a more helpless expression on Nick's face. Striding toward the two women, who were still standing on the step leading to the old doctor's study, she extended her hand. "I'm Brittany Matthews and I own this boarding house. Did I hear your friend call you Gussie?" she asked the woman clutching a coonskin cap.

Gussie nodded, but it was the taller woman who answered.

"I'm Adeline O'Hare—you can call me Addie—and this is my sister, Gretchen."

Brittany smiled. "I apologize for not being home when you arrived, but I thought you said you'd be here tomorrow at the earliest."

"We did," Adeline said through pursed lips that were painted bright red. "But Gretchen here couldn't wait another day."

"Oh, Gretchen-smetchen. My friends call me Gussie and you know it." Turning to Brittany, she said, "Ever since we won the lottery she's been trying to change me. If I've told her once, I've told her a million—make that two million, once for every dollar we won—times, I'm still the same old Gussie on the inside."

Addie released a long-suffering sigh. "If you're so intent upon remaining unchanged, why did you dye your hair?"

Gussie's blue eyes grew large with indignation, her hands going to her ample hips. "This is my natural color. At least it was until the gray took over. We couldn't very well come to a town that advertised for women without looking our best, now could we?" Turning to Brittany once again, she said, "The ad *did* say the men of Jasper Gulch needed women of *all* ages. There are single men our age, aren't there?"

Reaching for the suitcases at the ladies' feet, Nick said, "How young a man are you looking for?"

"Well, now, let's see. I'm forty-nine. Ow." Gussie rubbed her arm where Addie had so rudely jabbed her.

Raising her round chin, Addie said, "Gussie's *fifty*-nine and I'm sixty-one. As you can see, I'm the honest O'Hare sister. *Are* there single men our age here?"

Addie might have been honest, Brittany thought to herself as she tried to imagine the reactions of some of the older shy but willing Jasper Gents, but she was no less hopeful than her sister. Nodding, Brittany said, "There are several single men in your age bracket, and something tells me you two are going to make a lasting impression on each and every one of them.

Now, if you'd like to come this way, I'll show you the boarding house and help get you settled into your rooms."

Nick gestured for the women to precede him around the side of the house. Addie kept her eyes trained straight ahead as she traipsed past him, but Gussie eyed him all the way. "If you're not one of the cowboys who advertised for women, who are you?" she asked.

"I'm Nick Colter, Brittany's husband," he answered from behind. "I'm here to try to convince her to let me retain that position."

"Oh, my. How romantic."

Nick was aware that the older women were looking at him, but he was more interested in the expression on Brittany's face. He'd always thought she was pretty, but when she got her hackles up, she was a sight to behold. Her chin came up and her shoulders went back and her brown eyes glittered with petulance. Staying one step ahead of her always kept him on his toes. It revitalized him, and on a good day it made him feel like strutting. Today was turning out to be a very good day, indeed.

"See, Addie," Gussie declared, "I told you this was the place for us."

"Yes, sister, I believe you might be right." And the two walked into the house.

While Brittany showed the new boarders around the first level, Nick carried their suitcases upstairs. When he returned, Gussie and Addie were in the study and Brittany was in the kitchen brewing a pot of tea.

He entered the room quietly. From his position near the doorway he wondered how long it would take Brittany to notice his presence. Without moving or making a sound, he took a moment to look at her. Her navy sweater stopped a few inches above her hips and was loose enough to accommodate his hands should he have the opportunity to glide them around her waist. Her jeans were navy, too, but they clung to the smooth curve of her hips and the enticing shape of her—

He swallowed and forced his gaze higher, where wisps of dark brown hair waved over her collar. Clearing his throat, he said, "Is that tea for them or for you?"

She swung around, and with just one look, he could tell she knew what watching her had done to him. "It's for Addie and Gussie. You can have a cup if you'd like. Who knows? It might relax you."

Nick made a universally masculine sound, then turned on his heel. The only way tea would help him was if she laced it with whiskey.

"Where are you going?" she called to his back.

"To get the locks I bought in Pierre this morning. If I'm going to protect you and Savannah and a houseful of boarders, I'd better get busy."

"Can it wait a few minutes, Nick?"

He faced her slowly. "Maybe."

She glanced across the expanse of two rooms where the O'Hare sisters were looking at the books on the shelves in the old doctor's study. Keeping her eyes trained on the eccentric women, she said, "I have a few more things to do to get their rooms ready, and I was hoping you would entertain them for me."

"You want me to entertain Attila the Hun and her sister?"

Brittany was halted by the edge in his voice. "If you're nice to them," she said, trying not to laugh, "they'll be nice to you in return."

"That's what I'm afraid of."

This time she laughed out loud. "Oh, Nick."

He ran a hand through his hair and kneaded the muscles in the back of his neck. By the time he looked at her again, his eyes had darkened to the color of smoke. "All right. I'll entertain Addie and Gussie. On one condition."

"What condition?"

A hint of boldness found its way to his smile. "That you promise to 'Oh, Nick' me later, and take me with you to your historic society meeting tomorrow night."

Brittany crossed her arms and stared at him. "That's two conditions."

"I'm not surprised you noticed."

Something very close to happiness played around the edges of her mind. With a grin tugging at her mouth and the tingle of excitement walking across her heart, she felt at once young and very aware of what it meant to be a woman.

"All right. You win. You're welcome to sit in on the historic society meeting tomorrow night."

He took a step toward her. "And that other condition?"

"I think we should take one condition at a time, don't you?" Glancing at her watch, she said, "Besides, I have to pick up Savannah in fifteen minutes."

"I'll go. Really. I don't mind."

Grinning more than a nice woman should, she said, "All right. In the meantime you can keep Addie and Gussie entertained."

"What do you want me to do with them?"

"Charm them. After all, you can be very charming when you put your mind to it."

"You really think so?"

She turned her attention back to the tea. "Why don't you ask Gussie? Oh, and try not to point your gun at her coonskin cap."

"Just be glad I didn't twist her arm behind her back and haul her up against the building."

Lifting the tea bags from the steaming pot, Brittany glanced at Nick. "Something tells me Gussie would have liked that, but I have to say you're definitely making progress."

Nick ambled closer as if he was sure of himself and his rightful place in the universe. "I told you I've changed."

His blue eyes shimmered with light from the window, but it was the light coming from within him that held her still as he took the tray of tea and headed into the next room. She didn't know how long she stood in the kitchen, dazed, but by the time she'd made her way upstairs and had taken the sheets and blankets from the closet in the hall, she was smiling. She'd been doing that a lot lately. Nobody else had ever made her smile like Nick did. Remembering the change that had come over him in the diner earlier, when he'd asked how long Melody Carson had been married, Brittany reminded herself that nobody had ever made her cry like he had, either.

The Jasper Gulch Historic Society meeting had been called to order nearly an hour ago. As far as Nick could tell, there had been nothing orderly about anything since. From what he'd seen so far they should have called it the Jasper Gulch Gossip Society. Most of the nine members seated in Brittany's study were of the gray-haired set. Isabell Pruitt was by far the noisiest. She'd spent the first thirty-eight minutes discussing the disparaging decline of morals in the world in general and in Jasper Gulch in particular. Brittany had tried to bring the conversation to the history of the area, but Isabell was more interested in the indignity she and the other fine, upstanding citizens of Jasper Gulch had suffered the night the punch had been spiked.

Nick had a feeling the old bat was more upset about the fact that she hadn't caught whoever was responsible in the act. He thought about mentioning it, but as the only person present containing a Y chromosome, he already stuck out like a sore thumb. Rather than call more attention to himself, he sat in a straight-backed chair near the door and kept quiet.

Isabell made a show of peering into the living room. She eyed the dark hallway at the top of the stairs and wrinkled up her nose. In a voice reminiscent of fingernails on a chalkboard, she said, "Did your new boarders go out for the evening, Brittany?"

Brittany nodded, and for the eighth time—Nick was counting—she tried to turn the conversation to history. "Have you ever seen the journal Jasper Carson kept, chronicling his early days in Jasper Gulch?"

As a new member of the Carson family, Melody started to

answer. Unfortunately, Isabell beat her to the draw and waved the question aside. "Did anybody see the way those two new women were dressed today? Goodness gracious, they looked like a neon sign. For what, I can only shudder."

"Do you mean—" Opal gasped.

"If I've said it once," Isabell sputtered, "I've said it a hundred times. Women of ill repute, that's the kind of women that advertisement will lure to our fine town."

"Be careful," Melody warned. "That ad brought Brittany here. Besides, I think Addie and Gussie are a little too old to be women of ill repute."

Isabell raised what little chin she had and exclaimed, "From what I hear *some* women are never too old. But of course I would never include Brittany in that description. Why, she's been like a breath of fresh air to our quiet town."

Nick stared at Brittany, unmoving. Leaning down to hear something Edith Ferguson was saying, she had a tray of cookies in her hands and a smile on her face. He'd never seen the brown dress she was wearing, and he couldn't remember the last time he'd heard her laugh that way. She looked very Western in her wide belt and long, gathered skirt. She also looked very—what?

Happy.

The thought froze in his brain while a familiar ache settled in his chest. Brittany was happy. It's what he'd always wanted her to be, and what he'd never quite been able to accomplish. God knows he'd tried, and in the early days of their marriage things had seemed all right. Not perfect. Hell, he could never give her the kind of life her father had given her. When money was tight, Nick had worked double shifts. Money was tight a lot. Brittany had never complained about their financial situation, but he was proud and stubborn and dammit, he wanted to give her a better life. A better house, better car, safety and security. He failed on every count.

Opal was making a tsk, tsk sound, and Mertyl was nodding thoughtfully. Nick drew one ankle up to rest on his other knee.

Within seconds he lowered his foot to the floor again and leaned back in his chair. All this sitting around was driving him crazy. He felt agitated, trapped. He needed to do something. Better yet, he needed to arrest somebody.

Edith Ferguson, the widow who lived across the street, dabbed at her forehead with an old-fashioned lace handkerchief. "I parked behind their car this morning, and I could hardly believe what the sign on their bumper said. If You Can Read This, Follow Me. What sort of women use such deplorable tactics to get a man?"

Nick glanced around the room. Opal was shaking her head. Sitting next to her, Louetta looked decidedly ill at ease. Before he could come up with an explanation for the younger Graham's quietude, a woman who'd introduced herself as Norma Zammeron piped up and said, "I wasn't going to mention this, but I happened to glance at the cars and trucks parked in front of the Crazy Horse on my way by and guess whose Cadillac I saw?"

Nick just bet the old hen wasn't going to mention it. He was in the process of scowling when somebody on the other side of the room said, "What kind of a woman drives all the way from Illinois wearing a coonskin cap?"

"An eccentric one."

"An odd one."

"Downright strange is more like it."

"And desperate."

"My, yes, definitely desperate."

"Maybe Gussie and Addie are just lonely," Brittany said quietly.

Eight pairs of eyes turned to Brittany, only to flutter slightly before settling on a button or a purse or a speck of lint in their laps. Something shifted in the very center of Nick. Despite their gossiping ways, these women seemed to have a genuine respect for Brittany. That wasn't surprising. She'd always made friends easily. That's why he'd never understood how she could have been lonely in Chicago. She could talk to peo-

le in line at the grocery store or in the middle of the mall,
andering into conversations with anybody and everybody she
et. This was different. She didn't wander into idle conver-
ation with these people. They'd opened their narrow minds
d had accepted her into their community. She wasn't lonely
ere.

These days Nick understood a lot more about loneliness. In
e six months Brittany and Savannah had been gone he'd
njoyed an occasional beer or a White Sox or Bears game
ith some of the guys on the force. He'd always gone home
any empty house he'd once shared with the only woman in
e world who had a smile that could seep past his weariness
the end of a long, hard day, a woman who had a deep,
iltry laugh and a touch that could send need sparking through
m like lightning.

A shrill whistle nearly split Nick's eardrums. Several of the
omen winced and complained to Melody Carson, but the
ond-haired woman only grinned. "Thank you, ladies," she
id as if using a two-fingered whistle to claim the floor was
everyday occurrence. "I've been talking to my sister-in-
w about something, and I'd like to run it past you."

"By all means tell us what it is," Mertyl said, as if it was
omehow Melody's fault for taking so long to bring up some-
ing worthwhile.

Resting one hand along the top of her round abdomen, Mel-
dy said, "I know we're a new society, but I think we're
apable of big things. I'd like our first effort to be the staging
an 1890s wedding ceremony. We'll need to do some re-
earch, but the church was built about that time, and I know
r a fact that Reverend Jones has a prayer book dating back
that era."

"Why, Melody," Isabell exclaimed, "I think that's a mar-
lous idea."

"Yes, yes, indeed," Opal agreed. "In fact, I think we
ould include it in our annual Founder's Day celebration."

"But that's in less than two weeks!" Edith declared.

"Can you think of a better way to show the citizens Jasper Gulch what a fine organization we are?" Opal asked

The society warmed to the topic, asking questions, makin comments. A committee was formed, votes were cast, an plans for the first annual Jasper Gulch Historic Society staged 1890s wedding were launched.

"We'll have to go through the trunks in our attics in ord to find clothes suitable to wear to such an event," Edith sai

"I have just the thing!" Norma Zammeron exclaimed.

Nick noticed the exchange of meaningful glances betwee Melody and Brittany. At Brittany's nod, Melody sai "DoraLee has a wedding gown that belonged to her grea grandmother. I know she'd let us borrow it for the day."

Isabell wrinkled up her nose. "Off the record, I wou rather not have to ask that woman to borrow the dress."

As if on cue, Brittany said, "There's no need for you to that, Isabell." Isabell was in the middle of grinning when Br tany continued. "I'd be happy to ask her on behalf of t entire Jasper Gulch Historic Society."

Isabell's grin faded. Short of coming right out and sayin she simply didn't approve of the woman who owned t town's only bar, there wasn't much she could do. A feeli very close to awe squeezed into Nick's chest. He'd alwa known Brittany was bright, but the way she handled the people was amazing. She'd moved around a lot when she w growing up, rarely ending a school year in the same city had begun. Despite all the upheaval, she'd graduated fro high school at the top of her class. She'd been attending co lege before Savannah had been born. If it hadn't been for hi Brittany would have obtained a degree in history or cryptolo or something else she loved. Who knows where she mig have gone and what she might have become—if she'd nev met him.

Brittany was in the middle of laughing at Melody Carson seedy joke when she glanced across the room at Nick. He w looking at her, his jaw set, his mouth closed tight, his shou

ers squared. Her laughter leaked out of her until there was
only a small smile on her face. He returned a smile of sorts,
but it didn't reach his eyes.

She tried to tell herself he was just moody. She reminded
herself that he'd never been very good at sitting still. But she
couldn't shake the feeling that she'd witnessed the expression
on his face before.

Doubts niggled at the back of her mind throughout the rest
of the meeting. They remained with her even after the meeting
had been adjourned and half the members had gone, but it
wasn't until Nick had excused himself to go check on Savan-
ah that she understood what was wrong.

Opal Graham patted Brittany on the back and said, "That
man moves as if he owns the ground he walks on, doesn't he?
I know my Louetta would like to find a man a little like your
Nicholas."

Hearing Nick referred to as "her Nicholas" caused her
breath to catch in her throat. Brittany tried not to dwell on the
feeling that he'd never really been hers, concentrating instead
on the fact that Opal didn't seem to be aware that Louetta had
met *and entertained* a man last weekend.

Brittany glanced up, straight into Louetta's gray eyes. The
tall, slender woman had obviously overheard her mother's
comment. Although she followed Opal out the door, she
wasn't blushing. It seemed that there was more to Louetta
Graham than met the eye.

Within minutes, everyone was gone. Eyes closed, Brittany
rested her forehead against the door and sighed. Nick was the
one with the sixth sense about danger, yet she knew before
he turned around that he'd entered the room.

He was standing near the stairs, arms folded, eyes on her.
"That was some group."

"Yeah. You should hear what Crystal has to say about the
group dynamics of these little social gatherings."

He didn't laugh. He didn't even smile. Wanting to understand what had put the distant look in his eyes and the tension in his shoulders, she strode closer. "Nick, what's wrong?"

He circled to the right, kneading a knot in the back of his neck. "DoraLee warned me that small-town people were notorious for their preoccupation with strangers and gossip."

"The people of Jasper Gulch gossip about everybody, strangers and locals alike."

"How nice of them."

She turned her head, keeping him in her line of vision. "They are nice, Nick."

He paced to the sofa, to the chair, to the kitchen doorway. "Great. Keeping *nice* people safe is always more nerve-racking than keeping lowlifes safe."

"Is that why you're so restless tonight?"

The shrug he gave her made her want to reach out and touch him. "Inactivity drives me crazy."

"Waiting is always difficult."

"What do you say we get out of here?" he said. "Let's go to the Crazy Horse so you can ask DoraLee about borrowing her great-grandmother's wedding dress before old Isabell comes up with a reason not to."

"It didn't take you long to figure Isabell out."

"What do you say?" he asked.

"You want to go to the Crazy Horse now?"

"There's no time like the present. Crystal will watch Savannah if we ask her. Come on, Brittany. Let's get out of here and have a little fun."

"You were always good at talking me into doing something I shouldn't."

A muscle worked in his cheek. "Is that a yes or a no?"

"You're also very persistent."

"I'm a hard man to love. I know."

Brittany raised her eyes to his. Although they hadn't said 'I love you' in years, she wanted to tell him he was easy to love. She wanted to tell him she'd never stopped loving him, but that particular Pandora's box was better left untouched. So he touched him, the pads of three fingers slowly circling his mouth, angling his chin down. She reached up on tiptoe, pressing her lips to his. He closed his eyes and held very still. She heard his breath catch, felt the rumble of his restraint. He didn't wrap his arms around her or move in any way. He just held her kiss like a man who was savoring something very precious.

One second a knock sounded on the door, and the next second they jerked apart. "Are you expecting company?" he asked.

The slight shake of her head had Nick reaching for his gun. Damn. He'd left it upstairs in the closet.

"Who is it?" he called.

"It's me, er, Louetta Graham. I seem to have left my purse. May I come in?"

Nick heard Brittany's breath whoosh out of her. "It's not Dawson. Thank God."

While she went to open the door, he marched into the old study. They'd both recovered from their moment of fear, but what Nick was feeling at that moment was even worse. Brittany shouldn't have to be afraid every time somebody knocked on her door. If it wasn't for him, she wouldn't be. Hell, if it wasn't for him, she would have married some wealthy college graduate her father would have approved of. They would have had two point five children and would be living in a ritzy suburb where the biggest concerns were saving the whooping crane or the rain forest or the hump-backed whale. Honorable, safe aspirations.

Louetta and Brittany were talking in the next room. Retrieving a shiny black purse from the desk, he turned on his heel and retraced his footsteps. "Here," he said, dropping the purse into Louetta's hand.

"Oh, um, thank you." Glancing from him to Brittany, Louetta said, "I didn't mean to interrupt. It's just that I'd like to talk to Brittany in private. It'll only take a few minutes."

Nick didn't need to consult a psychic to know what was

coming. He clenched his jaw, and sure enough Brittany said, "Nick, why don't you go on to the Crazy Horse without me?"

He stared at Brittany. He was fully aware that Louetta Graham was watching him, but he didn't care. He didn't want to go to the Crazy Horse alone, dammit. They'd overreacted to the knock on the door. It was highly unlikely that Dawson would show up in Jasper Gulch. But if he did, the town's only bar would be the kind of place he'd go to nose around.

Brittany crossed her arms and redistributed her weight to one foot, but she didn't back down. When had she gotten so good at saying no without opening her mouth? Not just no. Absolutely-not-no. Maybe it would be better if he checked out the bar first. "I guess you could meet me there later. We could feed some quarters to the jukebox. And talk."

Without waiting for her answer, he grabbed his coat off the rack and walked out the door.

Brittany didn't know why she suddenly felt lonely. She wasn't alone. Louetta was here in this very room. Savannah was sleeping in her bed in the little room in the back of the house, and Crystal and Mertyl were upstairs. Still, the entire house seemed strangely quiet. And strangely empty.

"I felt that way after Burke left, too."

Brittany glanced up, startled, because she hadn't spoken out loud. "Are my feelings that obvious?" she asked.

A telltale blush tinged Louetta's cheeks. Although it appeared to require a great deal of effort, she loosened the death grip she had on her purse and heaved a great sigh. "I'm hardly qualified to offer advice, but every man doesn't look at every woman the way your husband looked at you a few moments ago."

Brittany closed her eyes against the moisture gathering there. Opening them again, she said, "Would you like to sit down?"

Louetta's graceful dip into the overstuffed chair was at odds with her starched skirt, flat shoes and unbecoming hairstyle.

Brittany had seen Louetta often these past six months. They'd exchanged greetings and smiles, but they'd rarely spoken. The woman sitting across from her looked very different from the woman Brittany and Nick had encountered in the alley behind the diner on Sunday. Then, Louetta's hair had been long and loose, her body covered by a thin blue robe. Tonight, her hair was pulled back in a tight bun, her clothing something her mother had probably chosen. Only her eyes looked the same. A deep, stormy gray, they were rimmed with dark lashes and filled with an intensity Brittany was only now beginning to recognize.

Louetta bit her lower lip, her fingers clasped tightly together. "You're probably thinking it's strange that a mousy old maid like me still blushes like a teenager."

Leaning ahead in her chair, Brittany whispered, "I was thinking that you have beautiful eyes."

Soft thoughts shaped Louetta's smile as she said, "That's what Burke said."

Her blush darkened until they both laughed.

"Your mother doesn't know about him, does she?" Brittany asked.

Louetta shook her head.

"And you didn't really forget your purse, did you?"

Again Louetta shook her head. "I left it here so I would have a reason to come back without Mother."

"I won't say anything to anyone, Louetta."

Fiddling with the clasp on her purse, Louetta said, "It isn't that I'm ashamed of what I did. I'm not. I've never met a man like Burke, and I've never felt like this. It's just that my father died when I was very young. Mother raised me by herself, and she's, well, she's very protective of me. I don't want to hurt her, so I'm going to wait until Burke comes back to tell her about him. About us."

Brittany hadn't realized she'd placed her hand on Louetta's arm until the other woman glanced down at it. "Then he's coming back?" Brittany asked.

"He has business to take care of in Oklahoma, but he's coming back in two months. Maybe less." The light in Louetta's eyes dared Brittany to question Burke Kincaid's sincerity.

"If it's any consolation," Brittany said, softening her words with a smile, "it's been ten years since Nick swept me off my feet, and I still haven't fully recovered my equilibrium."

Louetta rose to her feet and started toward the door. "I don't *want* to recover my equilibrium. I never want to stop feeling this way."

Brittany thought about Louetta long after she'd closed the door behind her. After checking on Savannah, she wandered back out to the living room and proceeded to glide her hand along the back of the sofa and along the windowsill where her flowers bloomed in vases filled with water. The crocuses were still lovely, but the daffodils were beginning to fade. In a week the petals would dry up and the bulbs would be dormant until next year when they bloomed all over again.

She felt a little like those flowers, lying dormant while she waited for love to bloom in Nick's heart. The tulips in the last vase were the same color as the blush that had crept to Louetta's cheeks a few minutes ago. Louetta thought of herself as an old maid, yet she was in the spring of her life. If Louetta was brave enough to allow her love to bloom for a virtual stranger, maybe it was time Brittany stopped trying to shore her heart against the man she'd fallen in love with all those years ago. In the very least she could meet him at the Crazy Horse to talk.

She hurried up the stairs before she could change her mind. Pausing only long enough to listen for Crystal to answer her knock, she poked her head into her friend's room. "I'm sorry to bother you, Crystal, but would you do me a favor?"

From her lotus position on the floor, Crystal answered without opening her eyes. "Aummm. Aummm. Naaaame it."

"Would you keep an eye on Savannah while I go to the Crazy Horse?"

"Aummm. I'd be happy tooooo."

"Thanks, Crystal. Keep the doors locked, Okay? I won't be late."

The chanting stopped, and one of Crystal's eyes opened. "Stay as late as you want. But Brittany? You're blushing. Have you been taking lessons from Louetta?"

Brittany backed from the room, her hands automatically going to her face. Crystal was right. Her cheeks *were* warm. Far deeper she felt as if something was blooming. Why, it felt a little like a daffodil bravely raising its face toward the sun.

Chapter Seven

Two nights ago the Crazy Horse had been relatively quiet. Tonight, the place was booming. There was popcorn on the floor and cowboys and ranchers everywhere. Even the music playing on the jukebox was louder tonight. Cletus McCully and his cronies were sitting at their usual table, and Forrest Wilkie and his friends were huddled around theirs. Gussie and Addie looked a little forlorn sitting all by themselves. Seated at the bar, where he was in plain view of the door, Nick could relate.

"A watched pot never boils, sugar."

Scowling, Nick swirled his untouched beer. DoraLee's cheeks and forehead were shiny from all the bustling around she'd been doing. Leaning her elbows on the bar, she met his stare as if she found a perverse pleasure in the challenge in his eyes. Shaking his head, he said, "Women around here are mighty stubborn, you know that DoraLee?"

"I could say the same for the men."

With his thumb he traced a path in the condensation on the outside of his beer bottle. "Yeah, well, the men around here don't seem to trust me any more than Brittany does."

"These boys just don't appreciate another man in town, that's all. They'll come around. I don't know why Brittany doesn't trust you. I guess you're the only one who can answer that one."

Somebody in the back of the room called for another round. DoraLee bustled away with a tray of long-necked bottles, leaving Nick alone with his thoughts once again. For crying out loud, it wasn't like he'd come here in answer to some silly advertisement. But he supposed DoraLee had a point. Maybe the good old boys of Jasper Gulch would come around once he'd earned their trust. He wasn't so sure about Brittany.

There was nothing new about that. He'd never been completely sure of her and he'd sure as blazes never been certain of the reason their marriage had ended. At the time, the night those burglars had broken into their house had felt like the beginning of the end. He should have been there that night. Hell, he should have been there a lot of nights. He'd lost Brittany one late night, one missed dinner, one difficult choice at a time. Work had gotten in the way too many times to count. She'd tried to be understanding, but he would never forget the look on her face when she had come back from her father's funeral, alone. He'd closed in on the biggest drug ring in Chicago that day. Some of the worst dregs of the earth were behind bars as a result of that bust. He'd been a hero around the precinct, and a failure as a husband.

The hair on the back of his neck stood up—a sure sign that somebody was watching him. He swiveled around on the bar stool and unerringly met Cletus McCully's open stare.

The old man gave his cigar a few puffs before slowly rising to his feet. Nick slid off his stool about the same time Cletus stopped in front of him. Hooking a thumb through one suspender, Cletus gave him a thorough once-over. "You look like hell, boy. Me and a few of the locals have just the thing for what ails you."

"I doubt that, Cletus."

That knowing grin set Nick's teeth on edge. Taking another

long puff on his smelly cigar, the stoop-shouldered old cowboy said, "Hold on there, young fella, until you've heard me out. See that mechanical bull over in the corner? DoraLee used to rent one just like it every summer before rodeo season. I happened to see this old relic at an auction last week. I got it for a song and sung it myself. Donated it to the Crazy Horse for the good of the entire community. The Ladies Aid Society doesn't exactly see it that way, but the boys have been having a high old time riding it. A couple of 'em wanna see you try."

Without another word he turned his back on Nick and ambled away. Nick had a lot of pride and a fair amount of curiosity, but neither of those things were the reason he followed Cletus to a table in the center of the room. Boredom was responsible for that. Boredom had gotten a lot of men into trouble over the years.

Clutching the cigar between two gnarled old fingers, Cletus said, "Forrest here would like to make you a little wager."

Nick eyed the sandy-haired rancher. Forrest Wilkie sent Nick a hostile glare.

"Do you have a problem with me, Forrest?"

Another man answered. "Forrest didn't say that. We were just wondering what a gal like Brittany sees in a man she's divorcing, when she's got all us cowboys to choose from."

It required every ounce of restraint Nick possessed to keep from responding to the loudmouth's condescending attitude. Keeping his eyes open and his voice steady, he said, "Forrest and I have met. Who are you?"

Nick enjoyed a moment of satisfaction as the other man flushed. Recovering, the rancher smoothed a finger over his mustache, puffed up his chest and squared his shoulders. "I'm Rory O'Grady. It just so happens the O'Gradys own the biggest spread in this part of South Dakota."

Nick nodded. "I imagine it takes a lot of work to run a ranch. Why don't you just say whatever it is you want to say."

Cletus slapped Nick on the back with enough force to knock

the wind out of him. "Didn't I tell you boys he ain't half-bad? Ooo-eee, this is starting to get interesting."

"I don't know about that," Forrest protested.

"That's right," Rory agreed. "The man's not stupid, I'll give him that, but I still don't think a cop from Chicago has anything to offer a woman like Brittany that a man out here can't top."

Nick's throat convulsed on a swallow, his fingers curling into fists at his side. "She married me, didn't she?"

"Yeah," Forrest countered, slowly rising to his feet. "And I hear tell she's divorcing you, too. I've been waitin' all winter for her to take her weddin' ring off. As soon as she does, I'm plannin' on making my move."

Cletus stepped between Nick and Forrest. "Easy, boys. I think you're gettin' a little off the subject." Eyeing the two men facing off across the narrow expanse of one small table, he said, "There's two ways to settle this. With your fists or by puttin' your money where your mouth is and placin' the seat of your pants on that there bull."

Nick looked at the mechanical bull, at Cletus, at Rory and Forrest. He'd faced hardened criminals who'd left him less speechless than these three men. "You want me to ride that thing?"

"What's the matter?" Forrest asked. "Don't you think you can do it?"

"I didn't say that."

With the snap of one suspender, Cletus slapped Nick on the back again and said, "I knew you'd see it my way. Forrest, you go first. Don't worry, Nick old boy, my money's on you."

Imposing an iron will upon himself, Nick clamped his mouth shut and glanced at the only man at the table who hadn't spoken. "You allow betting around here, Sheriff?"

Wyatt McCully tipped his white Stetson up with one finger and leaned back in his chair. "As long as it's harmless, I've been known to turn a blind eye and a deaf ear. In this case

I'd say it's better than a fist fight. Who knows, it might do everybody some good.''

The two lawmen's gazes held, each sizing up the other. There were squint lines beside Wyatt McCully's eyes, but it was the steadiness of his gaze that caused Nick to change his initial assessment of the sheriff of Jones County. Perhaps Cletus McCully's grandson was good at a few things other than helping little old ladies cross the street and rescuing kittens out of trees.

Forrest took his time rising to his feet. Amidst dozens of shouts, he hoisted himself onto the saddle in the center of the mechanical bull. The contraption began to move, swaying in one direction and bucking in another. The man rode like a pro. Hell, he'd probably competed in dozens of rodeos over the years. Nick hadn't even been on a horse since he was a kid. He didn't know how he'd gotten himself into this, but it looked as if there was only one way out. His father always said his pride was going to be his downfall. It was going to take a lot more than pride to keep his butt in that saddle.

Much too soon, the mechanical bull slowed and came to a stop. Forrest jumped to the floor to a chorus of yee-ha's. Cletus placed his hand on Nick's shoulder. "You can do it, boy. Just keep your feet in the stirrups and your mind on the gal you married and all the reasons you're tryin' to keep her. Now up you go. Easy does it.''

From the saddle, Nick glanced at the door one last time. Disappointment grated on his nerves. Looking around the room, the disappointment moved over to make room for a fair amount of unease. All eyes were on him. Most of the people in the bar were probably waiting for him to fall on his face. Or worse.

Clenching his teeth, he signaled to Cletus to start the ride. The bull began to move. Nick concentrated on keeping his balance. He would move with it, dammit, or die trying. He saw a blur of faces, heard a whir of raised voices, but he focused on the nuts and bolts that were jerking and pulsating underneath him. He wasn't a rancher or a cowboy, and maybe he couldn't give Brittany the simple life that they could offer her. But by God he would stay on this beast if it was the last thing he ever did.

He only wished Brittany had bothered to show up to see it.

By the time the mechanical bull slowed and finally came to a stop, Nick's head was spinning. Sliding to the floor, he realized his head was the least of his worries. His legs shook, his knees wobbled, every joint ached, and his teeth felt as if they'd been rattled loose.

When he was relatively certain he could stand on his own, he let go of the steel contraption and glanced around. Several five-dollar bills exchanged hands, and several more cowboys shook their heads. Cletus was grinning, though, and so were Gussie and Addie and DoraLee. He caught a movement out of the corner of his eye. Turning his head, his knees went weak all over again.

Brittany was standing near the bar on the other side of the room. Her eyes were in shadow, but he knew their color by heart. She was still wearing the brown dress and the wide leather belt that made her look very Western, very feminine. A murmur went through the crowd. It seemed Nick wasn't the only one who was waiting to see what she would do.

Brittany was aware of the low rumbling and grumbling going on all around her. Making her way through the throng of cowboys and ranchers blocking her path, she couldn't take her eyes off Nick.

He was different from the men out here. It was a difference that would have shown up even if he tried to disguise it with boots and a worn cowboy hat. Not that Nick would ever do that. He was who he was—a policeman who'd grown up with an older brother who'd taught him how to survive on streets that were unsafe and in alleys where anything could happen. Because of it or in spite of it, Nick moved with a smooth efficiency the men who had been born and raised out here simply didn't have.

Staring at the firm line of his jaw and the shallow cleft in his chin, it seemed ironic that she'd moved to a place smack dab in the middle of lean, rugged cowboys who looked darn good in Levi's and pointy-toed boots, yet the only man she'd ever wanted wore scuffed loafers and faded cotton shirts that had seen better days.

"You came." The words rushed out of him on a loud breath that was part relief, part pleasure.

Brittany nodded. "I'll never understand what possesses men to do some of the things they do."

He took another step toward her and said, "Forrest and Rory had a score to settle with me. Cletus thought a bull ride would be more effective than a fist fight. I didn't think you were going to come. I'm glad you did."

She had no intention of leaning closer, but her nose picked up the faint scent of his skin, a masculine, earthy scent that made her eyelashes flutter down and her lungs draw in a shaky breath. By the time she realized what was happening, her face was very close to his, and her heartbeat had slowed to match her thoughts.

She glanced to the right of Nick's shoulder where Cletus McCully was nodding and grinning for no apparent reason. It reminded her that she and Nick weren't alone. "Are you having fun?" she asked.

"I am now. What did you think of my ride?"

He'd spoken close to her ear. When she looked at him again, she couldn't help smiling. "I wouldn't hit the rodeo circuit just yet if I were you."

Nick regarded Brittany quizzically for a moment. He was a man, with a man-sized ego. Although he'd never had a problem with self-esteem or an overly exaggerated sense of self-worth, he'd never had to go searching for compliments, either. Suddenly he wondered how his jeans looked from the back, compared with these taut, rugged cowboys. He squeezed his eyes shut in an effort to dispel that particular mental picture.

"Nick, are you in pain?"

He opened his eyes and considered Brittany's question. "You could say that. Can I buy you a drink?"

They both turned toward the commotion on the other side of the room. Gussie and Addie had Cletus cornered by the jukebox. Nearly everyone was talking at once, and poor DoraLee was running off her feet trying to keep up with calls for more rounds of beer.

Brittany said, "It's pretty noisy here. Maybe we should go someplace quieter."

Nick's heart thudded and his breathing slowed. Someplace quieter? One place came to mind.

They were out on the sidewalk in no time. Anxious to be alone with her, he looked up and down the street for her car. As if reading his mind, she said, "I walked. That's what took me so long."

"Don't do that again."

The edge in Nick's voice had come out of nowhere. Looking at him over the top of his car, she said, "Don't do what again?"

"I don't want you or Savannah to walk anyplace by yourselves. Day or night. I'm pretty sure it's me Dawson wants, but he'll use you to get to me if he has to."

Brittany was quiet during the ride to the boarding house. She couldn't help it. She agreed with Nick's logic, but the simple fact that he'd mentioned Dawson's name brought the real reason he'd come to Jasper Gulch to the front of her mind. She was almost certain they could get to the heart of their problems if he could get past his feelings of responsibility and duty. But how could they accomplish that with the threat of Dawson hanging over their heads?

She unlocked the door with her new key and was hanging up her coat when she heard Nick slide the bolt into place once again. "Nick?" she asked, slowly turning to face him. "What are your plans?"

"My plans?" The coat he'd been in the process of hanging next to hers fell to the floor, forgotten. His hands went to her shoulders, warming her through the soft fabric of her dress. "I was thinking of taking you to a quiet room where I could draw the shades and dim the lights and lower the zipper down the back of that dress."

He was standing so close she could feel the heat from his body. Barely able to raise her voice above a hoarse whisper, she said, "That isn't what I meant."

His eyes were trained on her mouth as if he was thinking very seriously about kissing her. "Maybe you should tell me what you meant before it's too late for either of us to do much talking."

His meaning was clear, his intention obvious. Both sent a slow burn through Brittany that was making it very difficult to think, let alone speak. Trying valiantly to keep a clear head, she said, "I want to know about your plans for the future."

He answered without hesitation, his words rolling off his tongue. "Let's see. Now that Forrest Wilkie has seen the writing on the wall where you're concerned, I guess I won't have to flatten his nose anytime soon."

Brittany wondered when she would learn not to be surprised by this unpredictable man. She tried to glare at him indignantly but ended up shaking her head. "If there was ever anything between us, it was in Forrest's mind. I talked to him a couple of times, that's all. He's rugged and tough. He'll get over it."

"You think Forrest is rugged?" he asked, his voice sharp, his eyes blazing.

She merely stared, tongue-tied. She had no idea why he looked and sounded so angry. She didn't understand him. What else was new? Brushing her hair out of her eyes, she said, "Did I miss something here? I thought we were talking about your plans."

"My plans."

"Yes. You know, for the future."

He looked baffled. In his defense, she doubted that he understood her any better than she understood him. "Well," he said, stalling. "I'd like to visit my parents in Florida. I'd like to travel a little. Jake and I always talked about starting our own business after we capture the last crook on the streets. In the meantime, I want you in my bed. I know that's where we got into trouble in the beginning. And I don't want to get you in trouble again."

Brittany stared at him. She tried to be angry. At the very least she should have taken offense, because everything always came back to sex and the reason he'd married her in the first place. She'd been pregnant—in trouble was what he'd called it. But his expression was so darned sincere it melted away her anger. In its place there was only a burgeoning kind of hope that reminded her of Louetta and spring flowers.

"What are you trying to say, Nick? That you want me, but you aren't going to allow things to get out of control until we're sure it's the right thing to do?"

Nick opened his mouth to speak. No sound came. He didn't know what he'd been trying to say, but it sure as hell wasn't that.

"Because I think that's a marvelous idea. Things have always been explosive between us, and you're right. That *is* how we got into trouble when we were young. This threat of Dawson hanging over our heads makes everything feel more intense, more dangerous, more tempting. He's the reason you're here. Maybe we should use this opportunity to spend time together without the added complication of sex. We've never tried that before."

Nick ran a hand over his eyes, down his face, across his chin. Of course they'd never tried that before. There was a good reason for that fact.

He didn't know what to say. She acted as if this was his idea. If she knew him at all, she would know better. "Hell," he muttered under his breath. He wondered if she would have reached a similar conclusion if he'd been one of her *rugged* cowboys.

"What did you say? I couldn't hear you. Nick, are you all right?"

The sound he made was universal and all male. No, he wasn't all right. He was agitated and frustrated as hell. He had good reason. He was a man, dammit. A married man. A married man who didn't have much choice but to play this her way. "I'm fine. I think I'll go on up to bed now." He took the stairs two at a time.

"Nick?"

He stopped on the sixth stair.

Brittany was looking up at him. Arms folded, she tilted her head slightly and said, "I just figured out what you said under your breath a few moments ago. As far as I'm concerned, no man looks better walking away than you do."

Her smile hit him right between the eyes. He might have returned the grin, but he would never be sure. He took the remaining stairs, opened his door, flipped on his light and pulled the shade. Kicking off his shoes, he yanked his shirt over his head and headed for the bathroom at the end of the hall.

He stared at his reflection in the mirror over the old-fashioned sink. *She likes the way your jeans fit, Colter.*

Stripping out of his clothes, he stepped beneath the hot spray of the shower. Lathering up a washcloth, he scrubbed it over muscles that would be stiff tomorrow. Water, blessedly hot, sluiced down his body. He opened his mouth beneath the spray and laughed out loud.

Brittany liked the way he looked walking away. Maybe it was about time he proved that he could look even better walking toward her.

"Can we go shopping, Mommy?"

Brittany lowered herself into a chair at the table opposite

Savannah. "Since when do you like to go shopping, young lady?"

The little girl scrunched up her eyes and drew her shoulders as high as they would go. "Amy Stevenson and Jolene McKenzie are going shopping for new dresses to wear to the spring dance with their daddies. Even Haley Carson's going, and she thinks shopping's stupid."

Brittany smiled at the expression on Savannah's face. Her blue eyes were clear and bright. She had a dainty chin, skin that was pale and soft as only a young child's could be. Nick was convinced she was going to be a beauty someday. Brittany didn't care if Savannah never became model perfect. She rather liked the way her little girl looked with her missing front teeth and her hair tucked behind her ears. She looked normal, the tiniest bit impish and, most important, happy.

Savannah smiled often these days. It had a lot to do with this town, and a lot to do with her father's visit. Although Brittany hated the thought of her daughter's life being in danger, Savannah was thrilled that her father's stay coincided with the upcoming father-daughter dance.

"We can go shopping this afternoon after you get out of school," Brittany said.

Savannah smiled, then turned thoughtful. "Jeremy Everts is mad cuz Haley can go to the dance and he can't. On accounta he's a boy and all. Haley says they oughta have a mother-son dance just to make it fair. But I'm glad they don't."

"Why are you glad about that?" Brittany asked.

"Because then you couldn't go, cuz you don't have a little boy to go with. Haley's new mom is going to have a baby. Haley thinks it's gonna be a boy. I think you and daddy should have a baby, too."

"Savannah, honey, I don't think that would be a very good idea. Daddy only came for a visit."

The little girl looked up from her bowl of cereal. "He'd stay if you had another baby."

Savannah couldn't possibly know how close to the heart her

words had sliced. Nick chose that moment to saunter into the kitchen. His hair was sleep tousled, his face unshaven. He didn't appear any too chipper as his gaze settled on Brittany's, but he managed a small smile. Brittany couldn't believe how easy it was to smile in return.

"Daddy? Don't you want to put a baby in Mommy's tummy?"

Orange juice from the pitcher he'd been pouring ran over the top of his glass, pooling on the counter below. Swallowing, Brittany said, "Savannah and I were just talking about the father-daughter dance on Friday."

"And I was telling Mommy—"

"Finish your milk, Savannah," Nick growled.

The young girl's eyes grew large as if she wasn't accustomed to that tone in her father's voice. Doing as she was told, she finished her milk then slid off her chair. "Are you a grouch, Daddy?"

This time, it was Brittany who cut in. "Your father's just tired. Why don't you get your jacket so I can take you to school?"

Eyeing Nick as if he was a bomb that could go off any second, Savannah said, "Come help me, Mommy."

Nick felt outnumbered beneath Brittany's and Savannah's measured looks. When they'd left the room, he sopped up the spilled juice and scowled again. Savannah was right. He was ornery. He couldn't help it. He'd gotten almost no sleep and even less peace. He'd gone to bed with the best of intentions. He wanted Brittany to appreciate the sight of him walking toward her.

Good job, Colter. Showing her your ornery side is sure to work like a charm.

He reached for a frying pan and a carton of eggs. His mother always said feed a fever, starve a cold. He knew of only one remedy for what ailed him. And somehow Brittany had gotten the impression that he'd agreed to refrain from making love, in an effort to work out their problems.

Where was the logic in that? In bed was the only place he and Brittany had ever seen eye to eye. Face to face. Chest to chest. Thigh to thigh.

Hell.

He switched off the burner, turned on his heel and headed for the shower. This morning he would make it an ice-cold one.

The house was quiet when Brittany let herself in after taking Savannah to school. She stood at the bottom of the stairway, listening for a sign of Nick. The shower had been running when she'd left. Now, the upper level was silent. Crystal had gone to work, Mertyl would be up soon, but Gussie and Addie preferred to sleep until noon.

Mertyl's big, yellow cat slunk around the corner and plodded noisily down the stairs. Brittany followed Daisy into the kitchen where the cat began yowling to be fed. A piece of paper lying on the table drew her attention. Picking it up, she read the words written in Nick's messy scrawl.

"Sorry so ornery. Went for a walk. Be back soon to make amends."

She studied the words unhurriedly, letter by letter, the cat doing figure eights around her ankles. The thought of Nick traipsing through the quiet streets of Jasper Gulch put a smile on her face. No doubt the residents would be talking about it the rest of the day.

She heard the front door open and close. Strange, Nick was usually quieter than that. She turned around just as he walked into the kitchen.

"I see you got my note." He'd stopped in the doorway, one hand on his hip.

"Did your walk do you any good, Nick?"

Giving a nod of sorts, he strode closer and pulled a bouquet of spring flowers from behind his back. "These are for you."

"I didn't know my red tulips had bloomed."

"They haven't. You don't think I'd ruin your flower beds, do you?"

There was something warm and enchanting about the devilment in his eyes. Deciding she must have imagined his ominous sense of unease, she reached into a cupboard for a vase. "If these didn't come from my flower beds, where did you get them?"

"From a garden over on Oliver Street."

She spun around, clutching the vase to her chest. "Not Isabell Pruitt's garden."

He nodded largely and feigned innocence badly. "She caught me red-handed. Threatened to call the sheriff. Would have, too, if I hadn't happened to mention that I was picking them for you."

"Oh, Nick."

"Why don't you come here and say that?"

She almost did what he asked, catching herself in the nick of time.

"You really are going to be stubborn about this, aren't you?" he asked.

She carried the flowers to the table without answering. It wasn't until she'd placed them on the doily Mertyl had given her that Nick's silence drew her gaze once again. He'd strolled closer, the expression in his eyes as unreadable as stone. In the tight space so near him she couldn't think of a thing to say or do. He had no such problem. His breath whooshed out of him, warm on her cheek, his eyes holding her spellbound, his voice a husky whisper as he murmured her name. And then he kissed her. Not clumsy or awkward, but hungry and sincere.

His hand moved under her shirt, skimming across her back, slowly drawing her closer. The first brush of her body against his sent her emotions into a wild swirl. Fitting her body more intimately against his, she moaned his name.

His mouth moved over hers, his breath hot on her face, his

ands cupping and kneading. Hazy images danced through her
mind, images of taking his hand and strolling into her room.

He lifted his face from hers. And ended the kiss too soon.
Hours too soon.

There was something very unusual about that. Nick had
kissed her hundreds of times over the years, but she could
count on one hand the times he'd been the one to stop with
just a kiss. Raising her gaze to his, she said, "What's wrong?"

He regarded her quizzically for a moment. In a voice devoid
of all emotion, he said, "I talked to Jake while I was out.
Dawson's made a move."

A primitive warning sounded in her head. "What's he
done?"

She could sense the controlled power that was coiled inside
him as he reached for her hand. "Brittany, I—"

"Is everything all right in here?"

Brittany and Nick both turned their heads. Mertyl was peering at them from the doorway, her big yellow cat meowing to
be picked up.

"Yes, Mertyl," Brittany said, "everything's fine. Nick and
I were just talking, that's all."

"Would you excuse us?" Nick asked.

Without waiting for Mertyl's reply, he took Brittany's hand
and deftly strode through the living room and on into the old
doctor's study. Once there, they faced each other.

Brittany took a deep breath. And promptly closed the door.

Chapter Eight

Brittany tried not to notice the wariness in Nick's eyes. Sh[e] tried to tell herself a man who'd seen every kind of corruptic[n] would automatically react more strongly to the slightest threa[t] of danger. But this wasn't a slight threat of danger they wer[e] talking about. This was Kipp Dawson, a man who wouldn['t] think twice about killing a roomful of innocent people, a ma[n] who coerced eleven-year-old kids into working the streets fo[r] him, a man who'd gotten pregnant girls hooked on cocain[e] and heroine. Once, when Brittany had visited her mother i[n] the hospital, she'd seen a newborn baby who was goin[g] through withdrawals because of the mother's addiction t[o] drugs. That innocent child's suffering had haunted Brittany fo[r] years.

Nick's expression was every bit as haunting right now.

Drawing in a deep breath, she forbade herself to trembl[e.] "What have you learned, Nick?"

He opened his mouth, only to close it as if he didn't kno[w] where to begin. Finally he said, "I talked to Jake at the statio[n.] It seems somebody has broken into our apartment again."

Fear trickled down Brittany's spine. "Robbers?"

"Jake thinks it was Dawson's people."

"And you agree?"

Nick's nod was barely discernible. "Nothing was taken. And whoever did it practically signed Dawson's name."

"What did they leave?"

"Another copy of that magazine article. Underneath it was a copy of the newspaper clipping with Dawson's demand for a written apology from me crossed out."

Brittany's hands flew to her mouth. "What are we going to do?"

It was Nick's turn to take a shuddering breath. God, he hated this. He hated putting Brittany through this. Most of all, he hated the fear roiling in his stomach right now at the thought of what Dawson might do. Fighting to gain control of his ragged breathing, Nick uttered only one word. "We?"

She nodded, her eyes daring him to reject her help. The woman was barely five foot four and looked as if a strong wind could blow her into the next county. She'd always had a lot of spunk and she'd always tried to hide her fear from him. If it hadn't been for the way she was squeezing her hands into fists at her sides, she might have succeeded.

Nick strode to the window and peered out. It was hard to believe snow had blanketed the ground four days ago. The snow was but a memory, the sun bright in a pale blue sky, tufts of grass turning green before his eyes. A woman was hanging sheets on a clothesline next door. A puppy yipped on a back porch a yard away. It looked and sounded as peaceful as any other Wednesday morning in any other small town in the United States.

As far as he knew, Kipp Dawson wasn't planning a little trip to any other small town.

Nick started at the touch of Brittany's palm on his shoulder. Lowering his hand from the curtain, he said, "Guess I'm a little edgy."

"That's perfectly understandable. Now why don't you tell me what you think we should do."

He turned, the movement bringing his shoulder very clos
to hers. "I still think it's me Dawson wants. Not that he woul
show any remorse if you or Savannah got in his way. That'
why I'm going to keep both of you in my sight at all times.

She searched his eyes. For what, he wasn't certain. A lum
came and went in his throat. He wanted to crush her to him
to carry her up to his bed. Better yet, he wanted to take he
someplace far away. Someplace secluded and private and saf
He was familiar with the wish, and with the feelings of in
adequacy that always followed close on its heels.

Brittany had strolled to the bookshelves, talking as she ra
her fingers over the old leather bindings. "You're the one wit
the sixth sense and the insight as to what goes on in a crim
inal's mind. Do you think Dawson's nearby?"

On the other side of the room, Nick tested the new lock o
the door. Satisfied that it felt solid and secure, he said, "T
tell you the truth, I think he's toying with me. To him this i
nothing more than a game of cat and mouse. I want to chec
out the perimeters of the village and outlying areas, mayb
look for a place a man like Dawson might hide."

"Then we'd better check the sewer, Nick. Let's go."

"Let's?"

Once again she met his question with an open stare. Sh
was wearing faded blue jeans and a kelly green shirt tucke
in at the waist, the cuffs rolled up two or three times. He
clothes were of the working variety; her chin was set at
no-nonsense angle.

"Well?" she asked. "You said you wanted to spend tim
with me outside of bed. It looks as if you're going to kill tw
birds with one stone."

Nick clamped his mouth shut on the argument that arose i
response. First of all, *he'd* never said anything about stayin
out of her bed. Secondly, he wished she hadn't said *kill*. Re
fusing to give in to the jitters climbing up and down his spin
he opened the study door.

Mertyl almost fell into the room.

"For crying out loud," Nick sputtered. "Didn't anyone ever teach you that it's wrong to listen at the door?"

The frail old lady made a sound that was bigger than she was. "Soft as some people speak, it doesn't do a person much good to listen at the door, now does it?"

"Mertyl," Brittany said. "Do you think you could fix your own oatmeal this morning?"

The small woman rose to her full height. Eyes bright, she said, "I fixed my own breakfast for more than seventy years. Only let you do it for me because you seem to enjoy it. It's obvious you two want to be alone. Now go on. Get. And next time, speak up."

Nick and Brittany were both quiet as he pulled his car out of the driveway. Heading west over streets that had no signs, past yards that had countless places to hide, Nick said, "What do you think Mertyl would have done if she *had* overheard our conversation about Dawson?"

Staring out the window at houses whose curtains fluttered as she and Nick drove by, Brittany said, "Gossip travels faster than the speed of light in Jasper Gulch. If she'd heard us, every hunting rifle would have been cocked and ready by lunchtime."

Nick released an audible breath. "A hundred nervous trigger fingers would only make matters worse. I guess we should count our blessings that Mertyl's hard of hearing."

Brittany turned her head until she was staring at the stern lines of Nick's profile. His nose was straight, his chin square, his face made up of hard plains and masculine hollows. His eyes were his one feature that could soften his face, and his eyes were scanning the distance. He hadn't proclaimed his undying love for her. And yet he'd agreed to see her on her terms. Something shifted deep inside her. As the village limits gave way to rolling hills, she realized that she was doing as he said. Counting her blessings.

Ten minutes later Nick was steering around yet another crater-sized pothole in the county road. "I've already checked

out the elementary school," he said. "It has about as muc
security as the boarding house. The schoolyard is eve
worse."

"Maybe we should keep Savannah home," Brittany sai
quietly.

Nick neither nodded nor shook his head. "Before we d
that, I want to check out the area. For all we know, Dawsc
will never set foot on South Dakota soil, and after everythin
Savannah's been through, I don't want to disrupt her routir
unless we have to."

Brittany wondered how long Nick would stay if Dawsc
never showed up. She wondered if he could be happy in
town whose biggest crimes were gossip and jaywalking. A l
of men were content here.

Nick Colter wasn't a lot of men.

Leaning ahead slightly, she pointed to the first ranch the
came to. "This is Carson land. The shanty Jasper and Abiga
originally lived in was torn down years ago. Those big whi
houses were built by the next two generations. Clayt and Me
ody Carson live in one. Clayt's parents, Hugh and Rita, li
in the other."

Nick slowed the car to a crawl. Together they stared o
over land that stretched as far as the eye could see. Whi
fences surrounded a barn and lined a lane, small herds
brown cattle dotting the countryside.

Next, they came to an old iron bridge that spanned Sug
Creek. A drought had burned up most of the grazing grass
last summer, lowering the rivers and creeks to a mere trickl
Today the muddy water was almost level with the banks, tl
surface smooth and deceiving. Underneath, the current wou
undoubtedly be swift and treacherous.

The people who lived here had pasts that were riddled wi
stories of catastrophes, of droughts and drownings, of torn
does and locust plagues. This was a dangerous land, but the
dangers were nature's doing, not man-made. Again, Britta

wondered if Nick could be content away from the city, away from his brother, who also happened to be his best friend, away from crime and the surge of adrenaline that came from putting bad guys behind bars.

After a long stretch of silence, she said, "There are a hundred places for Dawson to hide out here."

Nick turned the corner very carefully and looked around. He'd been thinking the same thing. He'd lost track of how many times the hair on the back of his neck had stood up. There were sheds and shacks in the middle of nowhere, and houses that appeared to be empty. Dawson could have been hiding in any one of them.

"Look," Brittany said, pointing to an old run-down building with rotted steps and boarded-up windows. "That must be the old Grange Hall. I've heard about it, but this is the first time I've seen it."

Nick pulled the car onto a rutted lane that led to the weathered building. After taking careful note of every detail of the surrounding area, he opened his door, listening intently. Other than the wind and the chirruping of birds, the morning was quiet.

Meeting him around the front of the car, Brittany eyed the derelict building. "Too bad the historic society is penniless. This old Grange Hall would be worth preserving."

Nick could hardly believe his ears. He and Brittany were looking at the same building. Where he saw rotting boards and a sagging roof, she saw a piece of history. Her perceptions never ceased to amaze him. He viewed the world in black-and-white, good and evil, sin and retribution. She saw it in muted colors and shades of gray. Her views softened the jagged edges of his, just as her presence softened the jagged edges of his world.

She brought him to life. It was that simple. She made him want her in a way he'd never wanted anyone else. That wanting slowed his thoughts and deepened his breathing. It also made him yearn to give something back to her.

"Come on," he whispered, clasping her hand in his and drawing her with him around the side of the building.

"Where are we going?"

"Let's see if we can find a way inside."

"You want to break into the Grange Hall?"

She might have been trying to keep the excitement out of her voice, but he heard the energy in her whisper.

There were raccoon prints and deer tracks in the soft ground, but theirs were the only human footprints they saw. There was something exhilarating about that that made Brittany feel as if she was walking on untouched soil.

The spring breeze caught up with them behind the building. It fluttered the collar of Nick's coat, lifting his dark hair off his forehead. That same breeze was responsible for wending through her jacket and toying with the wispy tendrils of her own hair. "Nick," she said, whispering in reverence to the quiet morning, "the windows are all boarded up, and the doors are nailed shut. There's no way in."

Nick jiggled the metal handle on the door. Without warning, he slammed his shoulder against the door. Wood splintered and hinges creaked, but the door opened, intact. Gesturing with one hand, he said, "After you."

"We can't go inside. We're trespassing. Not to mention breaking and entering."

The ghost of an unholy grin lurked around the edges of Nick's mouth. "No we're not. We're investigating. Come on."

Brittany couldn't remember the last time she'd felt so giddy with excitement, but she remembered the first time. She'd been seventeen and had sneaked out of her house and met Nick at the end of the block. They'd taken the train downtown to Chicago. Hand in hand, they'd hiked the Magnificent Mile and strolled along Lake Michigan, eating hot dogs they'd gotten from a corner vender. It had all been innocent fun, really, yet that giddiness had stayed with her for days.

Similar feelings were shimmering through her right now,

Oh, she'd definitely been down this road before. She might have been able to resist the sensual lure of temptation, but the heady rush of wonder was too much for her.

She stepped over the threshold and sniffed the air.

The place smelled dank and musty. Once her eyes had adjusted to the dim interior, she saw rays of sunlight filtering through holes in the roof and slats in the sides of the building. Benches lined one side of the room; old oil lamps still hung on the walls.

"Just as I thought. Nobody's here but us."

Nick's voice came from a place close by. She glanced up and fell into the uncharacteristic playfulness in his expression. There was no doubt about it. The man was an ever-changing mystery. His eyes roamed her face, settling on her lips before slowly shifting lower. The tenderness in his features amazed her, but the hazy air of desire slowly enveloping them felt as natural as breathing.

"Isn't this place incredible?" Raising both arms to shoulder level, she tipped her head back, twirling in a circle.

Nick held perfectly still. This was his first glimpse of the young girl that was still inside Brittany. Even in the dim interior, her eyes were as bright as sunshine, her laughter as invigorating as summer rain.

She ended her twirl facing him, a look of wonder spreading across her features. His hand went to her shoulder, his voice a low rumble as he said, "You should have run away from me the first time you saw me."

She wet her lips, shrugged. "Maybe I should be running away right now."

Although he'd never know where he found the strength, he loosened his grip on her shoulder. "I wouldn't stop you, Brittany."

She looked up at him, unmoving. He noticed she wasn't running away. She wasn't even walking. She was standing before him in indecision the way she'd stood before him so many years ago. Suddenly, Nick didn't feel like a soon-to-be divorced man. Instead he felt like a man on the brink of a long-awaited honeymoon. He wanted to seize her weak moment and make love to her. Right here on the floor of the old building she loved, with bird song filtering through the roof and streaks of sunshine dappling the floor. Instead, he pulled the lapels of her jacket together and kissed her sweetly the way he had all those years ago.

Brittany's eyes closed and her breathing all but stopped. She didn't care. She didn't need to see or breathe. She only needed this connection with Nick. She touched his cheek, his shoulder, his chest, tentatively at first, but then, after he moaned, her memories took over, along with her instincts. She arched her back, bringing her body into contact with his, her thighs slipping between his, her stomach brushing the closure on his jeans.

He drew in a ragged breath, his lips leaving hers to skim the edge of her jaw and the soft skin at the base of her neck. "Uh, Brittany? If you're trying to test my willpower, it's working."

She straightened, her eyes searching his. "That wasn't a test, Nick. I just have a way of losing control when I'm with you."

He straightened, too. The shaky breath he took matched hers, but when he smiled, he could have knocked her over with a feather. "I'll take that as a compliment. But, Brittany, if we're going to go, we'd better do it soon."

She glanced toward the open door and then at the dusty interior of the room. "I guess our investigation is over. There's no sign of Dawson or anybody else."

Nick's voice slowed her progress toward the door. "I am sorry about this. I wanted to spend every waking moment with you. But not because of Dawson."

Brittany's feet were both on the ground, yet she felt as if she were perched on a narrow precipice, about to take a blind leap of faith. Turning in the doorway, she said, "I don't think we should allow Dawson to minimize or demoralize what's happening between us.''

"What *is* happening between us?"

"I'm not sure. I only know I like it. I like feeling giddy with anticipation at the thought of seeing you. I like the touch of your hand on my shoulder. I like spending time with you. Your time is something I've had very little of.''

Nick wasn't a man who was prone to sudden bursts of laughter, yet he was pretty sure he was about to do just that. Brittany liked him. She liked being with him. She liked being touched by him.

She was right about one thing. Time, measured in actual hours they'd spent together on a daily basis, was one thing that had been in very short supply during their marriage. Following her out into the sunshine, he said, "Maybe this is exactly what we needed, because I've got all the time in the world, and I'd like to spend every last minute of it with you. Not because of Dawson. Because of you.''

He closed the door and secured the latch with a combination lock he retrieved from his car. Eyeing the dilapidated structure, he said, "This lock probably isn't necessary, but I don't want to take any chances.''

A shiver danced down Brittany's spine. Starting toward the car, she wondered what kind of a chance she'd just taken with her heart. She raised her face into the breeze and concentrated on putting one foot in front of the other. She was still deeply in love with Nick. As long as there was a chance that he might love her in return there was no turning back.

"There," Brittany said, clicking a blue satin bow into place along the top of Savannah's head. "You look beautiful.''

Savannah waited to smile until after she'd turned this way and that in the full-length mirror. The new dress Brittany had bought for her at the Jasper Gulch Clothing Store had a big white collar and puffy sleeves. It reached below her knees and was tied at her waist with a wide satin sash. The dress, tights and patent leather shoes had cost Brittany nearly as much as she charged for a week's room and board. The smile on Savannah's face was worth every penny.

Tipping her head to one side and planting her hands on her narrow little hips, the child said, "Is this the kind of bow Shirley Temple would wear?"

Brittany brushed her finger over the tip of Savannah's pert nose. The child had been watching old movies all week. As a result, she wanted curly hair and tap dancing lessons. Her hair was fine and naturally straight. Brittany gave the curls in the long tresses half an hour, tops. Until tonight, she hadn't given much thought to dance lessons.

A wolf whistle preceded Nick into the room. "Who in the world is this ravishing creature?"

Savannah giggled behind her hand. Twirling around, she said, "Do I look like Shirley Temple?"

"Way better than Shirley."

"Oh, Daddy."

He held out his arm. "Come along, Your Highness. Your carriage awaits."

Reaching as high as she could for a six-year-old who was on the short side, she tucked her hand in the crook of Nick's arm. "What's a carriage?"

Nick's voice rumbled, a little tender, a lot warm. "It's a horse-drawn buggy for rich people."

"Are we rich, Daddy?"

His gaze strayed to Brittany's, a vaguely sensuous light passing between them. "I'm feeling rich these days. What do you think, Brittany?"

Brittany wended her way around Savannah's bed. Reaching up to fix Nick's tie, she said, "I think all the spare time you've had on your hands has gone to your head."

She felt his throat convulse beneath the knot of his tie. "Ah, Brittany. Spare time hasn't gone to my head. You have."

His skin looked tanned next to the white collar of his dress shirt. He'd shaved twice that day. He'd even let Ed give him a *regular* haircut down at the local barbershop. She knew, because they'd spent nearly every minute together.

No matter which room she happened to be in, Nick was there. He'd fixed the leaky faucet in the upstairs bathroom when she'd been trying to clean the sink. He'd been in daily contact with the men in his precinct in Chicago, relaying anything he learned the second he hung up the phone. He'd replaced the broken lock on the laundry room window while she'd put sheets in the washer. He'd been around so much Daisy had stopped yowling every time he entered a room. Mertyl still eyed him suspiciously, but secretly the old lady had admitted that she liked him. Gussie and Addie didn't even try to keep their feelings for him a secret. The two ample-bosomed sisters literally glowed every time he was near.

Brittany only hoped her reaction to him wasn't quite so obvious.

She'd lost track of how many times he'd kissed her these past three days. He'd touched her often, too, in passing and in passion, murmuring her name and his need. So far he hadn't said anything about love.

"What do you think, Brittany?" he asked.

Although it required a great deal of effort to pull her gaze away from his mouth, she took a step backward. Smoothing a loose curl away from Savannah's face, she said, "I think you two should get going. You don't want to be late."

"Goody!"

Brittany followed them to the front door where she bent to kiss Savannah's smooth cheek. "Aren't you going to kiss Daddy, too?"

Thinking things would be easier if her daughter was a little less bright and precocious, she reached on tiptoe to press a kiss to Nick's cheek.

"I'll see you later," he said, his breath a warm whisper on her face.

"Have fun," she called.

She was smiling when the door closed. As her smile drained

away, she told herself she had no reason to feel so bereft, no reason to feel as if time was running out. Nick had only gone for the evening. He would be back. *For how long?* she whispered to herself.

"Come on, kid," Crystal insisted, striding from the kitchen and hooking an arm through Brittany's. "Let's round up Gussie and Addie and Mertyl. You look as if you could use a few good friends."

"Is it *that* obvious?"

"What? That you still love him? It's obvious to me, but then, I studied body language in school."

Brittany cast her friend a sidelong glance. "There's really a class on that?"

"Would I lie?" Crystal probably couldn't help the fact that the glint in her green eyes wasn't very reassuring.

Allowing herself to be drawn into the kitchen, Brittany said, "In your educated opinion, what would you say Nick's body language is telling me?"

Crystal reached for the popcorn popper with one hand and the popcorn with the other. She set about her task, her bangle bracelets jangling on her arm, her gauzy shirt billowing as she moved. "That's a tough one. My professor always said, 'What men think, women feel.' I'm afraid thoughts are a lot harder to read than emotions."

"What if this Dawson business ends and I discover that Nick still doesn't really love me?"

Crystal turned around. This time there was no questioning the sincerity in her gaze. "Then you'll send him back to Chicago, you'll finally take off that wedding ring and you and Savannah will go on with your lives here just like you were doing before he came."

Brittany nodded slowly. Of course that was what she would do. She'd done it before. She could do it again. Couldn't she?

Rubbing her hands together, Crystal said, "What do you say we play a little poker tonight?"

"Since when do you like poker?"

With a lift of her delicately arched eyebrows, Crystal said, "Since Cletus showed me a new way to cheat. Don't tell Gussie and Addie."

Brittany was laughing before the first kernel of corn pinged against the lid. See? she said to herself. Her life could be very full without Nick.

It was strange the way that kind of fullness left such an empty feeling around her heart.

Brittany had been listening for the first rattle of the doorknob and had opened the door before Nick located his key. He strode inside, Savannah sound asleep on his shoulder. Her hair had gone straight, her sash was askew and her legs dangled limply beneath her father's strong arm.

"Did she make it all the way through the dance?" Brittany whispered.

"This kid's a socialite if I ever saw one. She didn't conk out until I pointed the car toward home."

He carried her down the short hall and into her bedroom. "Did you miss us?" he asked quietly.

Their gazes locked as they lowered Savannah to the bed, Brittany on one side of the narrow mattress, Nick on the other. "Actually," she said, "I've had a very interesting evening."

"Really."

As far as Nick was concerned, Brittany's smile lit up the room. Slipping Savannah's shoes off her feet, she nodded. "Crystal, Mertyl, Gussie, Addie and I played poker."

"Don't tell me. It was Crystal's idea."

"Cletus isn't the only one who cheats."

They were speaking in whispers, smiling in turn. Although Nick hovered close to the bed, it was Brittany's hands that removed the ribbon from Savannah's hair, Brittany's hands that sat Savannah up and deftly unfastened the buttons down the child's back. Nick could have watched those hands all night. Better yet, he longed to feel them flutter down his arm, spreading wide on his chest, skimming through his hair, down his back, along his waist, closing, grasping, working magic all night long.

It was probably a good thing that Savannah woke up, capturing Brittany's attention. Otherwise Nick might have swung Brittany into his arms and carried her into her bedroom next door.

Sleepily, Savannah helped her mother get her out of her party dress and into her flannel pajamas. Seconds after her head touched the pillow and her blankets were tucked beneath her chin, she was sound asleep all over again.

Nick met Brittany at the foot of the small bed. Their gazes met, held, only to slide away to gaze at their sleeping child. They both started toward the door in the same instant, as if propelled by the same need. In the narrow span of hallway that stretched between Savannah's room and Brittany's, Nick whispered, "How long are you going to make me wait?"

He heard her breath catch in her throat, saw her eyelashes flutter down. "As long as it takes."

"As long as what takes?" he asked.

She seemed to be fighting a battle within herself. When she finally spoke, it was in a hushed whisper. "As long as it takes to feel right."

Nick had no idea what she meant. As far as he was concerned, making love to Brittany had always felt right. He knew she wanted him. It was there in her eyes and in the vein pulsing in the delicate hollow at the base of her throat. She'd always wanted him. But she hadn't always been ready. He realized that now. When he was young, he'd rushed her. He was trying desperately not to rush her now.

Doing everything in his power to control the need that was growing stronger every day, he touched his forehead to hers and took a deep breath. "I learned something interesting tonight."

"About Dawson?"

He shook his head, slowly lifting his forehead from hers. "Much more interesting than him."

Brittany felt a smile coming on. And then, everything inside her went perfectly still. Her thoughts, her breathing, even her heart seemed to stop for one brief moment. She wasn't certain that staying out of Nick's bed was luring him any closer to love, but she was falling a little farther, a little harder every day.

It was his humor, brief and totally unexpected. It was his passion, strong and barely controlled. It was the way he walked, the way he talked, the way he smiled. It was everything about him. Only him.

Drawing away slightly, she said, "What interesting thing did you learn tonight?"

He waited to answer until they'd both entered the living room. Settling his weight along the back of the old sofa, he bent one knee and crossed his arms. "Opal, Isabell and Louetta served punch and cookies at the dance tonight. Good old Isabell is still trying to discover the identity of the person who spiked the punch at that wedding last week. She'll never find out, because she would never believe who did it."

The mystery in Nick's voice beckoned to Brittany, drawing her closer. "Do you know who did it?"

"I could tell you, but then I'd have to find a way to silence you."

Brittany's chin came up and her shoulders went back. "Very funny. Give me a hint."

Loosening the knot on his tie, he said, "Who had the most to gain by spiking the punch?"

"At first Isabell was convinced Haley Carson had done it."

"Savannah's friend? The thought that somebody could even think our daughter's friend would do such a thing makes me shudder, but it wasn't a little girl who spiked that punch."

"Who?" Brittany asked. "The local cowboys and ranchers?"

He shook his head. "Nah. They can get booze at the Crazy Horse any night of the week."

"Who then?" Brittany asked.

"Didn't I hear somewhere that Isabell and Opal hadn't spo
ken a word to each other for months until that night?"

Brittany nodded. "According to the grapevine, they've bee
best friends all their lives. Something happened months ag
to put a rift in their friendship. It had to do with one of th
new women who moved to town. Nobody knows exactly wha
was said or done. It's gone down in history as one of the best
kept secrets of Jasper Gulch."

Nick said, "They let bygones be bygones when they dis
covered that spiked punch. Who do you think wanted the tw
old friends to make up, more than anybody else?"

Brittany hesitated, barely able to murmur the name on th
tip of her tongue. "Louetta. Of course it was Louetta. She le
the reception early, but she must have stayed long enough t
spike the punch."

Nick leaned on the couch, his tie loosened, his collar ope
his gaze steady. "Shortly after that, Burke Kincaid ran out c
gas."

Brittany stared at him with wonder. "You're right," sh
said. "Opal and Isabell would never believe it."

"I think Louetta Graham is slowly but surely coming o
of her shell." Nick's eyes searched hers as his voice dippe
lower. "Something tells me this town will never perceive h
in the same way again."

The underlying sensuality in his words captivated Brittan
the image of the way Louetta had looked with Burke Kinca
flashing through her mind. Folding her arms and redistributir
her weight, she said, "For a policeman, you're very perce
tive."

He stood slowly. "For a man, you mean."

That wasn't what Brittany had meant. She wasn't like tho
women who had a sharp dislike for the opposite sex perm
nently imbedded in their brains. She had no superiority com
plex where they were concerned, and no inferiority comple
either. She liked most men and most women.

She loved Nick.

And she knew, before he took another step, that he w
going to kiss her.

Chapter Nine

Nick was going to kiss Brittany, but first he wanted to simply look at her. He took his time, lingering on the wispy tresses of her dark hair, following the curve of her jaw, the length of her neck, the shape of her breasts. Emotions stirred within him, igniting a desire that could easily burn out of control. Before he had a chance to act on that desire, an expression he'd seen a hundred times crossed her face, and she pulled away slightly, just as she'd done so often in the past.

He didn't understand her. He never had. If he pressed his advantage, he knew he could lure her into his arms. He'd taken her countless ways over the years, usually by storm. He'd always been pleased with his ability to ease the stiffness from her shoulders with a touch and a kiss planted just so. He hated to admit it, but now he realized that she was right. All that lovemaking had been damned incredible, but it hadn't been enough to hold their marriage together. Something had been missing. He wondered if it might have been trust.

"Don't worry, Brittany," he said, inching closer. "This won't go any farther than you want it to go."

She sighed as his mouth covered hers, her knit shirt bunch-

ing in his fingers, her skin warm beneath his hands. He kisse
her until he thought he would go crazy if he couldn't hav
her. And then he kissed her a little more.

Although it required every ounce of restraint he possesse
he straightened. She looked up at him, her brown eyes dew
and soft. It was all he could do to keep from kissing her a
over again.

Brittany stared at Nick, mesmerized. He really had the mo
amazing eyes, full of heat and seduction. It reminded her o
the way he'd looked on their wedding day. She'd been s
caught up in airy hopes and dreams that day that she hadn
fully understood the magnitude of what that look had mean
Her father hadn't been happy about the imminent marriage o
his youngest child, but he'd walked her down the aisle, the
stood aside as she placed her hand in Nick's. Her older siste
Janice, had been her maid of honor; Nick's only brother, Jak
was his best man.

"You're smiling," Nick said. "I'm taking that as a goo
sign."

"I was just thinking about the day we were married an
what your brother told you he would do to you if you so muc
as made me cry."

"He said he'd kick my butt all the way to Cleveland," Nic
said on a growl. "This from a man who's terrified of com
mitment. I'm not afraid of commitment, Brittany. You kno
I want you."

Brittany didn't answer. She couldn't. Nick had wanted h
ten years ago, and he wanted her now. But was he in lov
with her? Someday maybe she'd get her courage up enoug
to ask. For now, she reached up, skimming her hand dow
one side of his face. "He called tonight while you were gone.

She knew what the butterfly touch of her fingertips wa
doing to him, could hear it in his breathing and see it in h
absent expression as he said, "Who?"

She almost smiled. "Jake. He said the police in Pittsburg
have spotted a man fitting Dawson's description."

Nick took a quick, sharp breath. "What would Dawson be oing in Pittsburgh?"

"Jake couldn't be sure," Brittany said. "But he wondered Dawson might have decided to set up business out of the olter brothers' jurisdiction."

"If that happened, I'd feel sorry for the people in Pitts-urgh, but at least you and Savannah would be safe."

"And you would be free to go back to Chicago."

As their eyes met, she felt a shock go through her. His face ad paled, his voice, when it came, had faded, losing its steely lge. "When the threat of Dawson is over, I want you and avannah to go back to Chicago with me. We can buy a house the suburbs if you want. I'll even put up a picket fence and aint it white."

Brittany stared at him, silent and unmoving. Her composure ad never felt more fragile. Once again she was afraid time as running out. She'd wondered if Nick would ever consider aying in Jasper Gulch. Now she knew he wasn't contem-lating any such thing.

The strain of desire was taking its toll on his features. His noulders were rigid, his chin set, his face taut. A battle was king place inside him. She was fighting a similar one within erself.

"Brittany, I—"

Her breath burned in her lungs, the prolonged anticipation lmost unbearable. "Yes?" she whispered.

"I want you."

She felt a moment's squeezing hurt because that wasn't hat she'd hoped he was going to say. He was waiting for er to make the next move, and it was costing him dearly. Her eart turned over in response to the need in his eyes. And she new, if—when he left Jasper Gulch, she would never feel xactly this way again. In that moment she realized that time asn't running out. It was standing still.

Rising up on tiptoe, she placed a hand on either side of his

face and slowly brought her lips to his. "I want you, too, Nic
I've never stopped."

The house was so quiet she could hear the air whoosh c
of him. Everyone else was asleep. As he clasped her hand
his and led the way to her bedroom, she knew it would be
long time before she and Nick went to sleep.

The lamp by the bed was turned to its lowest setting,
dim bulb casting a hazy glow over everything it touched. F
ing her at the foot of her bed, he kissed her lips, her chin,
neck. She tipped her head back, her eyes drifting closed,
lips following the trail of his fingertips as he worked her b
tons free. Her shirt fell open, his hands covering her brea
through the satiny fabric of her bra.

His touch became more insistent, his breathing raspier.
glided her shirt from her shoulders, down her arms, then def
did away with her bra. The air felt cool where her clothes h
been. Opening her eyes, she found Nick's gaze on her expos
flesh.

"So beautiful," he whispered.

In that instant she felt beautiful and warm and desirab
And deeply in love. She glided his tie from his collar. Tossi
it over her shoulder, her fingers moved to the buttons on
white dress shirt. Within seconds the shirt fell to the flo
behind him. Her eyes took in the dark tan of his skin,
sparse hair on his chest, the ripple of muscle leading to
slacks slung low on his hips.

She spread her fingers wide, her palms skimming his sho
ders, coming together at the base of his neck, slowly movi
lower. He drew in a ragged breath, his fingers curling into fi
at his sides. Brittany's heart swelled with feeling, her fing
trembling as she reached for the front closure on his slacks

His hand covered hers, stilling her movements as his ey
caught hers. Feeling winsome, wanton almost, she smiled a
twined her arms around his neck. He made a sound deep
his throat. The next thing she knew, she was on her back
the soft quilt, Nick's body pressed tight to hers.

His hands were everywhere, his mouth constantly seeking hers. "It's been so long," he whispered, covering her breast with his palm. "Too long."

She moved beneath him, seeking, needing, pleasing. He worked the front closure of her slacks free as she unhooked his belt. Seemingly doing everything in his power to hold on to the last thread of his control, his eyes closed, his breath moist and warm on her cheek as he whispered, "You're still on the pill, aren't you?"

It took a moment for Brittany to surface enough to understand the question. After a tense silence, she shook her head. "I went off it when we separated. I didn't expect to need birth control anymore."

He groaned, his head falling forward, his eyes closing. "I promised myself I would never leave you unprotected again."

Brittany had to clear a lump from her throat in order to speak. This was hardly the time to broach such a subject, and yet she had to ask, "Are you sorry I got pregnant, Nick? Sorry we had Savannah?"

"God, no," he said vehemently. "I'd die for that little girl. I can't imagine my life without her, and yet I'm sorry I got you in trouble, sorry I ruined your life. I was old enough to know better, old enough to see to protection."

She could feel the intensity in his eyes and the heat emanating from his body. Biting her lip to keep it from trembling, she whispered, "You can't have it both ways, Nick. If we had used protection, we wouldn't have Savannah. And we wouldn't have gotten married."

There was a pounding in Nick's head, like a drum beating far away. His desire was strong, and Brittany was so close. One movement would join her to him and drown out the doubt pounding loudly inside his skull. One movement. One act. The same movement, the same act that had resulted in Savannah's conception.

His lips felt dry, his face brittle, his lungs burning from lack of oxygen and from the question he had to voice. "Then you

wouldn't have married me, Brittany, if Savannah hadn't be
on the way?''

She took far too long to answer. When she opened h
mouth to speak, her voice was only a whisper. ''I don't kno
Nick. I just don't know.''

His eyes practically sparked, a muscle working in his chee
''You don't know? Or you don't want to say? I can take tl
truth, dammit.''

Everything inside Brittany went perfectly still. She'd ask
herself these questions countless times in the past. She hadr
married him because she'd been pregnant. *That* had been *h*
reason. She'd married Nick because she'd loved him, a
she'd believed that he'd loved her, too. As the days had turn
into months, and the months had turned into years, she'd r
alized that love and responsibility were two very differe
things. Oh, she knew he'd wanted her on several levels. The
was his desire and his pride, his love for Savannah and h
sense of duty. But none of those things added up to love f
her.

Nick's leg felt heavy on hers, but not as heavy as her hea
as she slowly turned her head.

He jerked away from her as if he'd been slapped. Rollir
to his feet in one lithe movement, he faced her, nostrils flarin
eyes blazing. ''I guess a person who doesn't like answe
shouldn't ask questions.''

She pushed herself to a sitting position. ''Nick, try to u
derstand.''

''Oh, I think you've made yourself perfectly clear.''

Nick hated himself for putting the paleness on Brittany
face. Hell, hating himself was nothing new. She'd swung h
feet over the side of the bed, averting her face, but not befo
her eyes had searched his and slowly filled with pain. F
wanted to grasp her shoulders and shake her. ''Tell me wh
you're looking for, dammit, so I can find it and give it to you

Brittany recognized the coiled energy in Nick's movemen
She wished there was something she could do or say, son

miracle she could perform. But there was nothing, because no matter what he said, he couldn't bring love to the surface at will. No one could. He couldn't *try* to love her, and she would sooner die than have him pretend. Love was either there or it wasn't.

He cared about her. He always had. These past several days she'd sensed that he was close to falling in love with her. What was it her father used to say?

"Close only counted in horseshoes and hand grenades."

Being *almost* in love with her hadn't been enough before they'd separated. It wasn't enough now.

She reached for her blouse. Standing before him fully covered, she waited for the explosion. His face contorted, but the explosion never came. With jerky movements, he scooped his shirt off the floor and headed for the door.

For a man who could move like the wind, he sounded more like a herd of elephants taking to the stairs. After waiting for the ominous slam of his door, she went to bed alone.

She lay awake for a long time, listening to the wind moaning through the eaves, rattling shutters and lifting branches and twigs. A storm was brewing out on the plains.

The end of her marriage was very near.

Nick leaned in the kitchen doorway. Thunder rumbled overhead; raindrops bounced off the roof and sluiced down windowpanes. He'd poked his head inside Savannah's room a few minutes ago. She was sound asleep, all the dolls and stuffed animals she'd been playing with earlier lined up at the foot of her bed, their "broken" paws bandaged, their pretend cuts and bruises healed.

While making his usual check around the house, he'd discovered that Gussie and Addie hadn't arrived home from their trip into Pierre. Mertyl and Crystal must have retired to their rooms immediately after the historic society meeting ended. Maybe it was for the best that they'd all gone to their separate corners. Everybody had been snappy and snarly for days.

Mertyl claimed it was the smell of rain and the heaviness in the air. He happened to know there was more to the shift in moods in the Jasper Gulch Boarding House than a change in atmospheric pressure.

Four days had passed since he and Brittany had almost made love. *Almost* had become his least favorite word in the English language.

Brittany was in the kitchen right now. Standing at the sink, her back to him, she sighed. To Nick it sounded as if the entire house sighed with her.

"So, how was the historic society meeting?"

She spun around, her flowered skirt swishing around her knees, her hair falling into her eyes. Easing from his slouched position in the doorway, he loosened his grip on the bouquet of spring flowers in his hand and said, "Sorry. I didn't mean to startle you."

Her eyes softened, but the sorrow deep inside them didn't lessen as she said, "I know, Nick. You just have a way of sneaking up on me, that's all."

Heaving a sigh of his own, he ambled into the room and lowered his frame onto a hard kitchen chair. Lord he was tired. He'd been in daily contact with his brother in Chicago. Although there had been no further word concerning Dawson's whereabouts, Nick continued to scout the area in and around Jasper Gulch. He'd played a little poker down at the Crazy Horse and had taken long walks around the neighborhood with Savannah. Nothing he'd done should have left him exhausted. Running a hand through his hair, he knew this weariness was emotional, not physical. Part of it was due to this godawful waiting. Part of it was due to the knowledge that his divorce was going to become final in three days and there wasn't a single thing he could do about it.

Brittany rubbed the towel over a saucer long after it was dry. Realizing what she was doing, she placed the towel and saucer on the counter and simply looked at Nick. She'd become accustomed to his long stretches of silence years ago.

This was different. Tonight he didn't look lost in thought. He looked lost.

Her heart went out to him, but she couldn't help him, not without losing herself. Searching her mind for a safe topic of conversation, she said, "If every member of the historic society works around the clock, I think we might be prepared for the staged 1890s wedding by next week."

A furrow creased his forehead as he looked at her. "I thought the 1890s wedding was set to be staged in three days, not next week."

"It is." Her stab at humor elicited a sound that might have passed for laughter if she hadn't known him so well. "How about you?" she asked, trying to fill the silence. "How did the people at the town meeting react to your self-defense demonstration?"

The sound he made deep in his throat reminded her of the thunder rumbling overhead. "Some self-defense demonstration it turned out to be. Everything I tried to show them was met with argument."

Sitting down opposite him, Brittany said, "The good folk of Jasper Gulch weren't exactly open to your suggestions and self-defense tactics?"

Nick uttered a most unbecoming word. "They argued, everybody claiming to have a better way. At least we don't have to worry about eighty-one-year-old Maude Simpson. I was trying to show her how to jab an assailant in the eyes with her fingers or kick him where it counts when, out of the blue, she clobbered me with her purse."

Brittany lost the battle not to smile. "You don't say."

He met her small smile with a grin of sorts that almost made it to his eyes. "It was one of those hard leather numbers with pointed corners and a big metal clasp. It left bruises. Wanna see?"

Brittany knew better than to try to answer. Before her eyes, the smile drained from his face, his eyes never leaving hers. She thought he looked lonely sitting at her table, one hand kneading a knot at the back of his neck, the other holding a bouquet of pink, yellow and blue flowers. She wanted to go to him and put her arms around him and just hold him. She couldn't. Because she knew what would happen if she touched him. One touch would lead to another, and another would lead to a kiss, and sooner or later they would be swooning and sighing. And then they would make love. It would be incredible. Making love with Nick had always been incredible. But it wouldn't solve anything. If anything, it would make letting him go even harder.

She rose to her feet and strolled around the table. Being careful not to touch him, she pointed to the bouquet in his hand. "Did you pick those in Isabell's garden, too?"

He shook his head and cleared his throat. "I bought these from somebody named Josie in a little store on Main Street."

Brittany nodded. "Josie Callahan moved to town about the same time I did. A young widow, she expanded the dime store to include a flower shop and bakery. Did you want me to put your flowers in water?"

He handed her the flowers, but didn't readily release them. He wanted to say something. Evidently thinking better of it, he lowered his hand to the table and stood, slowly making his way toward the door.

"Nick?"

He stopped, but he didn't turn all the way around.

"Do you think we could call a truce?"

"For Savannah's sake?" he asked.

"For everyone's sake. Especially ours."

At first she didn't think he was going to answer. When he did, it was in a voice that was deep and bone weary. "All right, Brittany. We'll call a truce. For all our sakes."

Lightning streaked the windows, thunder shook the ground. Glancing out at the night, he said, "That's some storm."

Brittany put the flowers in water then took a candle out of the cupboard just in case. "Mertyl's been predicting it all week. Before she fell asleep, Savannah informed me that April showers bring May flowers.''

His smile looked stiff, but his voice was as deep and masculine as always as he said, "We should have named that kid Sunny instead of Savannah.... Is it just me, or does this weather remind you of thunderstorms we used to have in Chicago?"

She remembered one time years ago when a thunderstorm had left them without power for three days. She and Nick had lit candles and had danced around the kitchen to music only they could hear.

The lights in the boarding house flickered again. Placing the candle in a holder, she reminded herself that she couldn't allow herself to be distracted by romantic notions anymore. She and Nick had called a truce of sorts. It would be wise to stick to it. Setting the matches on the counter, she said, "Let's just hope this downpour doesn't bring flash floods."

Nick was well aware of the way Brittany had skirted the memories of that long-ago thunderstorm. She was looking to the future, not the past. As much as he dreaded it, one day soon he would have to do it, too. After another long stretch of silence, he said, "Once I have confirmation on Kipp Dawson's whereabouts, I'll be leaving Jasper Gulch, Brittany."

She managed to keep her hand from flying to her throat, but there was nothing she could do about her heart. "Do you have any idea when that will be?"

"It depends." His eyes had narrowed; his voice sounded tired. "I'm not going to take any chances, but it might be as early as this weekend. You'll probably be relieved to see me go."

Brittany didn't know what to say. She'd thought the same thing a few days ago. Why wouldn't she be relieved to see him go? She hadn't slept well in nearly two weeks because of him. She felt confused because of him. Worse, she felt fragile. She felt edgy, skittish, sad. All because of him. She *should* have been relieved. Letting him go, watching him go, was going to be the hardest thing she'd ever done.

Without another word she went back to the sink and her earlier task. The next time she looked, Nick had left the room.

Late-evening sunlight streamed through the stained-glass window, throwing an elongated patch of color onto the old church floor. Several members of the historic society were standing near the front pew, while the two men who'd been roped into helping with the staged event shifted from one foot to the other.

"All right, Forrest. You'll be standing right here."

"Yes, ma'am."

"And, Crystal, you'll be on his left."

"Why do I have to be the bride?"

"Because you're the only person who fits into the wedding dress. Now stop fidgeting," Isabell Pruitt admonished.

"I can't stop fidgeting. Even pretending to be a bride gives me the jitters. Tell you what I'll do. I'll alter the dress to fit Brittany. I'll work all night if I have to."

Brittany's gaze strayed across the aisle where Nick was sitting by himself. His eyes were narrowed and hooded, a muscle working in his jaw. Pulling her attention back to Crystal, her throat convulsed on a swallow. "You can't alter DoraLee's great-grandmother's wedding dress," she whispered. "Besides, I can't be the bride. Not on the day my divorce becomes final. Melody can't do it because she's six months pregnant, and Louetta is the only person who can play the church organ. You're the best woman for the job, Crystal."

"That's where you're wrong," Crystal muttered under her breath.

"Don' choo worry, girl," Cletus McCully said with a snap of one suspender. "I've been walkin' a lot of gals down the aisle since that ad came out in the papers. I'm gettin' good at it, even if this weddin' is only for show."

While Opal conferred with Reverend Jones, and Isabell

barked orders about where the flowers would be placed and what music would be used, Brittany glanced at Nick, who was slowly making his way toward her. Meeting him halfway, she clasped the side of a pew with one hand and stared at him, unmoving. There were lines beside his eyes and a deep groove in one lean cheek. She tried to speak, swallowed and tried again. "Are you leaving?"

"Tomorrow."

Brittany floundered. "Actually," she said, clearing her throat, "I was referring to tonight, and whether or not you're ready to take Savannah home."

"Sure. If that's what you want."

She didn't even know what she wanted anymore. "Savannah will like that," she said. "She'd like you to stay for the Founders' Day Celebration tomorrow, too."

If Nick hadn't been in church, he might have given in to the need to swear out loud. Folks had been talking about the upcoming Founders' Day Celebration all week. The Anderson Brothers, along with Jason Tucker, had been working on a number for their barbershop quartet for days. A group of teen-aged girls had been practicing their clogging in the room behind Mel's Diner. He'd heard that some of the old-timers were going to dress up as fur traders. Rumor had it that Gussie had even loaned Roy Everts her coonskin cap. Nick was certain it would be a sight to see. But he couldn't stay. Staying on in Jasper Gulch now would only prolong the agony. Everyone else fit in here. Nick wondered if he fit anywhere. At least back in Chicago his life had purpose. Without the threat of Dawson, he didn't belong here.

Since there was nothing left to say, he turned and made his way to the back of the church, where Savannah was playing with three other girls. "Let's go, Savannah."

All three little girls stopped what they were doing to look up at him. As if Savannah, too, knew there was nothing left to say, she placed her fingers in his.

"Hey, mister, you forgot Savannah's coat."

Nick accepted the small jacket from the girl's outstretched hand. Older than Savannah by two or three years, there was something regal about the girl, despite the spattering of freckles across her nose and the grass stains on her knees. Nick knew without asking that this was Haley Carson, the girl Savannah looked up to. It was obvious that Haley watched out for Savannah.

Nick ran a hand through his hair, down his face, over his chin. He didn't want some little kid to watch out for Savannah for him. That was his job. He took a deep breath and tried to get his anger under control. He was frustrated, that's all. He had no aces up his sleeve, no backup plan. Jake had called earlier with word that a positive identification of Dawson had been made in Pittsburgh. Pittsburgh was a long way from Chicago, and a world away from Jasper Gulch. So Dawson's threat had been menacing, but empty, after all. Nick would leave, and all their lives would go on. It just didn't feel that way to him.

The sun had dipped out of sight when Nick and Savannah pushed through the heavy church doors and started down the steps. His little girl remained quiet during the ride home. Standing on the boarding house's wide front porch, she finally said, "You aren't going to stay in Jasper Gulch, are you Daddy?"

A lump came and went in Nick's throat. "I'm a policeman, Savannah-banana. Jones County already has a sheriff and deputies. What would I do here?"

"You'd be my daddy."

Going down on his haunches, Nick took his daughter's narrow shoulders in his hands. "I'll be your daddy no matter where I am. I'll come back and visit, and I'll call every week. I promise."

Nick didn't blame Savannah for looking so forlorn. After all, his little speech had sounded empty even to him. That alone could have attributed to the hair that suddenly stood up on the back of his neck. He caught a movement out of the corner of his eye and glanced at the house across the street just in time to see a curtain flutter in one of the windows on the second floor.

Nick shook his head. It looked as if Edith Ferguson was spying on her neighbors again. Scowling, he unlocked Brittany's front door and took Savannah inside.

"So that's where you've been staying," the man muttered under his breath after jerking out of view.

From his position at the upstairs window, he could still see the house across the street. The white sign on the front porch stood out against the burgundy siding and black shutters. The Jasper Gulch Boarding House. How quaint. Street signs would have made it a little easier to find, but he hadn't minded the challenge. It was nice of the old lady who lived in this house to leave the porch light on for him and the door open. Idiot. Might as well leave a sign out front for burglars. "Gone for the evening. Help yourself to the good silver and heirloom jewelry."

The man caught his reflection in the dark window. Running a finger along the scar on his face, he narrowed his eyes and swore. Burglar? He wasn't a burglar. He was a businessman. And he was going to enjoy the business of watching the life drain out of that condescending, holier-than-thou cop who couldn't be bought at any price.

He thought about doing it right now, but it was almost dark, and he preferred to do this job in the light of day. Besides, the missus wasn't home. He smiled at his sinister reflection. Colter's wife wasn't his type, but he'd make an exception this once.

Patience, he said to himself. He'd gone through a lot of trouble to make it look as if he was in Pittsburgh. All so Colter wouldn't suspect anything. Everybody knew the surprise was the best part. That wasn't quite true, he thought to himself as he made his way down the steps and into the shadows. The surprise was part of it, but the look in Colter's eyes was going to be the best part of his entire plan.

Tomorrow would be soon enough.

Chapter Ten

Morning came too soon. Years too soon, as far as Nick was concerned. He'd thrown his few belongings into his suitcases and had said his goodbyes before everyone had left to see to the million and one last-minute details for the Founders' Day Celebration today. The warmth of Savannah's arms around his neck had left him feeling raw, but the quiver in Brittany's lips as she'd murmured, "Goodbye, Nick," had nearly sent him to his knees. Mertyl had dabbed at her eyes; Addie and Gussie had cried outright. Even Crystal had seemed genuinely sorry to see him go.

Nobody was sorrier than he.

The band was playing in the distance when he tossed his bags into the back seat of his car. Closing the door, he cast one last look at the burgundy house where Savannah and Brittany now lived. He'd stared at the same house two weeks ago. Then, his arrival had seemed necessary. Now he knew it had all been for nothing. Brittany and Savannah hadn't needed his protection after all.

Then why was dread burning a path down his spine?

He slid onto the driver's seat and started his car, his gaze falling upon a crayon drawing from Savannah. In the drawing, a stick woman and a stick child were waving at a man who was driving away in what appeared to be a blue box on wheels. Savannah always signed and dated all her artwork. This masterpiece had today's date. D-Day. The day his divorce became final.

A cold knot rose to his throat as he backed from the driveway. He tried to tell himself these feelings were normal. His mind listened, but his instincts balked.

What was wrong? What had he overlooked? Inching around a corner, he had no answer.

The main thoroughfare in Jasper Gulch was literally crawling with people. Children darted around adults who were decorating tables and setting up booths on street corners. Cletus McCully was sitting on a bench in front of the post office. From their stools underneath the barber pole, a couple of old-timers watched Nick drive by. A group of cowboys dressed in chaps and dusty Stetsons were practicing their roping skills on the sidewalk a little farther down the street. The scene was chaotic, but not menacing in any way.

Nick clenched his jaw so tight his teeth ached.

Face it, Colter. You just don't want to leave.

Maybe that was all it was. Maybe this tension would ease once he'd crossed Sugar Creek and was heading east. Maybe sometime before the next millennium he would get over the failure of his marriage.

Traffic was barely moving on Main Street. Gritting his teeth in annoyance, he swore he could have gotten down on his hands and knees and crawled faster than he was going right now. He had to come to a complete stop to keep from running over the high school marching band that had gathered in the middle of the street. He raised his hand to blow the horn, stopping in midair at the sight of the plain gold ring on his finger.

"Sugar?"

Nick jumped, only to find DoraLee leaning inside the window on the passenger side. "For crying out loud, DoraLee. Aren't there village ordinances against blocking traffic?"

"You think you'd feel better if you arrested the band? These kids are gonna be a while. Might as well pull into a parking space and make the best of the sunny morning. I'm holding down the fort at the diner today. Come on in. Coffee's on me."

Nick didn't want to follow DoraLee into the diner for a cup of coffee. He wanted—he didn't even know what he wanted—but if he didn't get moving pretty soon, he was going to climb out of his skin.

DoraLee seemed to understand, keeping up a steady prattle all the way inside. "Tempers have been high around here, let me tell you. Edith Ferguson just chewed me out for buttering her toast the wrong way. She left me a dollar tip and apologized, blaming her bad mood on the fact that she and a few of the other members of the Ladies Aid Society were here at the diner until midnight baking the wares they're gonna sell at the bake sale later on this afternoon."

DoraLee stopped talking to Nick long enough to tell a handful of customers that she'd be right with them. "Have a seat, sugar. I'll be right back with that coffee."

Nick didn't sit down. He hiked one worn loafer on the bottom rung of a chair and waited for his eyes to adjust to the dim interior. The voices coming from the back of the room sounded familiar, but it was the words themselves that made Nick increasingly uneasy.

"A person don't expect to come across poachers this time of year," Karl Hanson mumbled.

"That's true," Jed Harely agreed. "It's too muddy and the cattle are too rangy."

"You really think you got a glimpse of a poacher or a cattle rustler?" Jason Tucker asked.

"Either that or he was seeing things," Jed declared.

"My eyesight is twenty-twenty, and I know what I saw."

Nick lowered his foot from the stool. "Did I hear you say you saw a stranger around your place, Karl?"

Karl put his coffee cup down and peered at Nick long and hard before answering. "Coulda been a poacher. Whoever it was hugged the shadows. Wouldn't have seen him at all if the moon hadn't been full last night."

"Then you didn't get a good look at him?"

Karl shrugged. "He disappeared around the backside of the old Grange Hall so fast I couldn't make much out. At first I thought he had gray hair, but he didn't move like he was old, ya know?"

The image of silver hair and a jagged scar flashed through Nick's mind, a comment DoraLee had made earlier close on its heels. Edith Ferguson, the widow who lived across the street from the boarding house, had been out until all hours the previous night. If the old lady hadn't been home, who had fluttered the curtain in that upstairs window?

"Here you go, sugar."

The primitive warning in Nick's head all but wiped out the sound of DoraLee's voice. Leaving the coffee steaming on the counter, Nick pushed through the diner's front door with enough force to rattle it off its hinges. Nearly blinded by the sudden brightness, he headed for his car across the street.

"Colter, wait!"

Nick spun around, a flash of silver blurring before his eyes. He came to a stop inches from Sheriff McCully. "Does the name Kipp Dawson mean anything to you?" the sheriff asked.

Nick felt as if a hand had closed around his throat. "What do you know about Kipp Dawson?"

"I just took a call from a Jake Colter. Seems he's been trying to reach you all morning. The connection wasn't very good, but he said to tell you that the man in Pittsburgh wasn't Dawson. He mumbled something about gut instincts and co-incidences and hopping on a plane. I told him I'd make sure you got the message."

The blood drained out of Nick's face. Dawson wasn't in

Pittsburgh. And it hadn't been Edith Ferguson spying on him and Savannah last night. A gray-haired stranger had been spotted near the Grange Hall. Instincts and coincidences be damned. Dawson was here.

Wyatt McCully was standing directly in front of Nick, ready and waiting, the April sun glinting off his white hat. "It's time you told me what's going on, Colter."

Through the roaring din in his ears, Nick said, "I have to check on my wife and daughter. I'll explain on the way."

"We'll take the cruiser," was all the sheriff said.

In some far corner of his mind, Nick was aware of the noise and laughter going on around him, of the warm breeze on his face. But all his senses were on alert for a gunshot or a glimpse of silver hair.

"Where to?" the sheriff asked.

Meeting Wyatt McCully's assessing brown eyes over the top of the police car, Nick said, "Savannah and Brittany are at the church with the other members of the historic society."

Wyatt nodded, but he didn't speak again until after he'd pulled the cruiser out of the alley behind his office and was headed for Church Street. "Just what kind of a man is Kipp Dawson?"

Scanning every inch of every shadow they passed, Nick said, "He's an educated criminal. An animal, really. If there's money to be made illegally, he has a hand in it. Drugs, prostitution, extortion, bribery, murder. He's tried them all."

"What's he doing in Jasper Gulch?"

The levelness in the sheriff's voice drew Nick's gaze. Fighting the sense of inadequacy washing over him, Nick finally said, "He came to teach me a lesson."

"Then it's up to us to stop him."

For the first time since learning that Dawson was in town, Nick realized that he wasn't alone in this after all.

Wyatt pulled the cruiser to the curb in front of the old white church. A group of women and children were gathered on the steps. Old Isabell was barking orders, Louetta was looking decidedly ill at ease and Mertyl was conferring with another gray-haired woman. And in the midst of it all, Savannah was playing on the sidewalk with her friends while Brittany looked on, her back to the street.

Nick tried to decide what to do. Dawson was already in the area. Somewhere. That meant the clock was ticking. Nick wanted to keep Brittany and Savannah safe. His instincts told him there was safety in numbers. As long as Brittany and Savannah stayed in the crowd, they would be okay.

It was him Dawson wanted.

Keeping his eyes trained on the sunlight glinting off Brittany's dark hair, Nick said to Wyatt, "Karl Hanson saw a silver-haired stranger out by the old Grange Hall."

Seconds later the car was speeding toward the village limits. Neither of the lawmen said a word as the Grange Hall came into view. Wyatt stopped the car and cut the engine. As if on cue, both men felt for their guns, then slowly got out of the car.

Nick circled to the right of the building, Wyatt to the left. Finding fresh footprints in the rain-soaked ground, Nick drew his gun. Ever careful not to make a sound, he stepped into the open behind the building. A heartbeat later, Wyatt did the same.

Wyatt pointed to the tracks in the earth. Nick nodded, gesturing to the door. Or what had been a door when he and Brittany had visited the building. It lay in splinters on the floor, the lock still secured to the handle. Nick stepped over the threshold, his shoes crunching on bits of wood and dry twigs while Wyatt stood watch in the doorway.

Nick made a systematic check of the building. Finding it empty, he hurried back the way he'd come. "He's been here," he said, stepping out into the sunshine. "But he isn't here anymore."

"Do you have any idea where he could have gone?"

Nick's expression was one of mute wretchedness. Shaking

his head, he finally said, "I don't know, but if we don't find him first, I pity the poor soul who does."

Brittany took a key from her purse then stood staring at her hand. Adjusting the skirt of the 1890s costume she was wearing, she jostled a stack of books, an old-fashioned hat and her purse into her other arm, then ran a fingertip over the plain gold band circling her finger.

Nick was gone. Her divorce was final. It was over, all over.

Her fingers trembled as she slipped the ring over her knuckle and slowly slid it into the pocket of her floor-length skirt. She'd known this day was coming. Still, she hadn't been prepared for this wrenching sense of grief. With her eyes burning and her throat raw, she turned the key and entered her front door.

She told herself there was too much to be done to allow herself the luxury of giving in to the need to cry. Isabell needed candles, Crystal needed pins, and Cletus needed matches for his smelly cigars. There was a wedding cake to be picked up, a costume to be ironed, Savannah's lunch to prepare. Brittany would see to all of it. In a moment. Closing the door, she leaned back against it and rested her eyes.

A chill black silence engulfed her. There was no logical explanation for the primitive panic that worked its way over every inch of her body. She spun on her heel, ready to take flight.

Steely fingers closed around her upper arm. "You can't leave already. You just got here."

Brittany's eyes widened in horror at her first glimpse of a jagged scar. The man standing before her was of average height and build. His clothes looked expensive, his tan artificial. Silver hair was unusual for a man in his late thirties, but it was Kipp Dawson's cold, calculating eyes that made her truly afraid. "Oh, my God," she whispered.

Murder? Revenge? He looked capable of it. He looked capable of anything.

"So, you recognize me. I'm flattered, Brittany." There wa
nothing flattering about his smile.

One by one the items in Brittany's arms fell to the floor
She couldn't think. She couldn't move. She could barel
breathe.

She didn't allow herself to shrink from the cold gray o
Dawson's eyes, concentrating instead on the pain where hi
fingers were cutting into her flesh. He loosened his grip onl
slightly, bringing his other hand to her face. "That magazin
article didn't do you justice. It's a shame it took you so lon;
to come home. I would have enjoyed wiling away the hour
with you before that husband of yours returns."

Brittany couldn't control her flinch any more than she coul
control the revulsion that climbed to her throat like bile. Will
ing her legs to hold her up, she tried to think. *Nick*, sh
screamed inside her head. *What should I do?* But Nick wa
gone. It was up to her to save herself. But how?

When she first tried to speak, her words came out in a croak
and she had to try again. "Nick and I are divorced. He isn'
staying here anymore."

Dawson's eyes narrowed on her face. He appeared satisfie
that she was telling the truth, but a look of derision unlik
anything she'd ever seen crossed his face. "If he isn't stayin;
here, where is he?"

She bit her lip, her heart thumping madly. Mertyl would b
bringing Savannah home any minute. Brittany had to get Daw
son out of there before that happened.

"I said where is he?"

He twisted her arm behind her back. She gasped at the pain
With her face pressed against the door, she knew her onl
hope was to get Dawson out in public where someone migh
be able to help her. Taking a shuddering breath, she said
"He's a good man. Please don't hurt him."

"Hurt him. Why, I'm going to kill him, just like I kille(
that woman who wanted to testify against me. Killing Colte

is going to be more fun because I know how much he's going to hate having you watch. Now where is he?''

In that instant Brittany knew that she was dealing with a man who was no longer human. Relying on an inner strength she didn't know she possessed, she said, ''Nick is planning to watch the parade on Main Street before he leaves town.''

She squeezed her eyes shut, praying she didn't pay for that lie with her life. Dawson leaned into her, his cheek close to hers, his breath moist and sickening on her neck as he said, ''That's what he thinks. I didn't go to all this trouble to let him get away.''

For the first time that day, Brittany was glad that Nick had left Jasper Gulch. At least he was safe. Heaven help her, she had to find a way to escape, too.

Trying to remember everything her father had taught her about thinking with her head and not her emotions, she said, ''The Founders' Day Celebration is getting underway. They're expecting me to pick up the flowers and a cake from a little shop on Main Street. The people in this town react to everything by overreacting. There's no telling what they'll do or who they'll alert if I don't show up right on schedule.''

Dawson ran a hand down his cheek. ''We wouldn't want to disappoint the fine people of this town, now would we? Let's go. But don't try anything funny. If you do, I'll kill you, and then I'll go find your little girl.''

Brittany's breath solidified in her throat, and she stumbled. Dawson kept an iron grip on her wrist as he slid into his car and pulled her in after him. Shoving the barrel of a gun into her ribs, he instructed her to start the engine. She drove carefully over streets frequented by people who still cringed at violent movies and whose biggest crimes were jaywalking and gossip. Parking in front of Josie's Five & Dime, she took a series of short breaths for courage and said, ''This is it. This is where I'm supposed to pick up the cake.''

''At a dime store?'' he groused. ''Don't take me for a fool, Brittany.''

"It's not just a dime store. It's a bakery and a flower shop, too."

His gray eyes narrowed. "All right," he said, spying the homemade pastries in the window. "Let's go."

Brittany's knees shook as she climbed from the car. She had no idea what she was going to do. She only hoped that Josie Callahan would suspect that something was wrong and would contact Sheriff McCully.

The bell over the door jingled as Brittany and Dawson walked inside, Brittany's hopes falling the instant her gaze rested on the gray-haired woman who was manning the counter in Josie Callahan's absence. "Hello, Brittany," Isabell Pruitt said, peering at the man behind her with interest. "Who's your friend?"

Brittany bit her lip to keep it from trembling. "Hello, *Josie*. This is—"

"Kipp Dawson. I'm Brittany's cousin. Nice place you have here, Josie. Nice town."

Brittany prayed that Isabell would pick up on the fact that she'd called her by the wrong name without bringing it to Kipp's attention. At the very least, she hoped the old busybody would see through the veneer of Dawson's charm.

Isabell's eyebrows went up, and a toothy grin split her face as she shook Dawson's hand. Brittany wanted to cry out in frustration, in fear, in desolation. With her last spark of hope extinguished, she picked up the cake and started for the door.

"It was nice meeting you, Mr. Dawson," Isabell called from behind the counter. "Brittany, dear, you'll have to bring your cousin by the house this evening. You know how much my husband, Walter, loves company."

Brittany nodded woodenly. Keeping her face devoid of all emotion, she said, "That sounds nice. Um, goodbye."

She didn't have the luxury of closing her eyes and uttering a prayer, but hope sprang anew because everyone knew that Isabell Pruitt wasn't married, not to a man named Walter, nor to anyone. Maybe Brittany had a chance after all.

"All right," Dawson said in her ear the moment they set foot on the sidewalk out front. "Now let's go pay that husband of yours a little visit."

Brittany crossed the street where she placed the cake in the car just so, stalling as long as she possibly could. The rodeo ropers were gone, but the marching band got in the way on the sidewalk between the dime store and the Crazy Horse Saloon next door. She could feel Dawson's frustration in the grip of his fingers on her arm. When the marching band moved on down the sidewalk, a sense of dread unlike anything she'd ever experienced washed over her. This was it. She was out of diversions. She and Dawson were on their way to the Crazy Horse Saloon. There was no telling what he would do when he discovered she'd lied.

It took a moment for Brittany's eyes to adjust to the dim interior of the saloon. As was usual in a small town, everybody turned to see who was entering. Forrest Wilkie pulled at the brim of his hat. Jason Tucker, a young cowboy who worked on the Carson ranch, grinned and called, "Hey, Brittany. Pull up a chair and sit a spell."

A cowboy in the back of the room fed quarters into the jukebox. The twangy country song covered the quiet, but it didn't quiet Brittany's nerves. Her entire world felt out of kilter. She'd never been inside the bar at eleven o'clock on a Saturday morning, but surely it was unusually crowded today.

"Where is he?" Dawson's voice was menacing and razor sharp in her ear.

Brittany opened her mouth, but her tongue was so dry she couldn't speak. Nothing made sense, nothing seemed real. What were these cowboys doing here? And why weren't any of them nursing a beer?

"Kipp," she said, "I don't—"

A man wearing a brown cowboy hat turned around at the bar. "Hello, Brittany."

She staggered, half afraid she was seeing a ghost. But no ghost had eyes so blue or a voice so deep and resonant.

"Oh, God, Nick!"

Rising to his feet slowly, Nick's eyes never left Dawson's face, his entire being coiled and ready. "This is between you and me, Kipp. Let her go."

Like a shark on the scent of blood, Dawson's movements became frenzied. He jerked Brittany in front of him. Using her body as a shield, he pointed his gun at Nick's chest and set the trigger.

Brittany wanted to cover her eyes and her ears, but she barely had time to scream. One of the cowboys cracked a whip. And then there was an explosion of sound. After that everything seemed to move in slow motion. Dawson's gun slid across the floor; Nick lunged toward her. "Brittany, duck!"

Ignoring the pain shooting up her arm, Brittany went limp. A lasso shot out, hovering over Dawson's head. The man moved, as agile as a cat and far more cunning, diving, rolling, springing back to his feet an instant after he'd slid a tiny derringer pistol from his boot.

Nick dove for the gun. Dawson was faster, and Nick missed his mark. Coming to his feet, Nick knew from the expression on everyone's faces that Dawson had turned the tables on them all.

"All right, Colter," Dawson said, his voice as hard and cold as steel. "It's time for you and me and the little woman here to take a little drive."

The door burst open. A man bearing a striking resemblance to Nick practically flew inside. A gun fired. A woman screamed. Brittany was pretty sure it hadn't been her.

Nick dove again. This time he didn't miss, tackling Dawson to the floor. There was a scuffle, a series of thumps and bumps. And then Nick was hauling Dawson to his feet.

The song on the jukebox ended, the room becoming eerily quiet. A faint feminine voice wavered from the other side of the room. "Could somebody call 911?" Crystal asked, her blond hair tumbling around her shoulders. "I think I have a little problem."

Everyone turned to the woman whose green eyes were glazing over and whose blood was slowly soaking into the blouse of her 1890s wedding gown.

"Jake!" Brittany screamed. "She's going to faint."

Nick's brother caught Crystal before she could hit the floor. Two other men held Dawson while Wyatt snapped handcuffs into place. By the time Nick had made his way to Crystal, Brittany was holding a cloth over the wound on her friend's shoulder, and Crystal's eyes were open once again.

"Lord, Brittany," she whispered. "You didn't tell me there were two of them."

"You're going to be all right, Crystal." Brittany's whisper doubled as a prayer.

Somebody must have gone to get Doc Masey, because the old doctor burst through the door, huffing and puffing, Cletus McCully right behind him. Looking on as Doc went to work, Cletus snapped one suspender and proclaimed, "Jumpin' catfish, Crystal, you'd do anything to get out of being the bride in today's mock weddin', wouldn't ya?"

Wetting her lips, Crystal said, "It looks as if you're going to have to play the part after all, Brittany."

Brittany truly knew how it felt to laugh and cry at the same time. Doc Masey determined that the wound to Crystal's shoulder wasn't as serious as it looked and instructed Jake, a total stranger, to carry the young woman to his office around the corner. Nick, Brittany and a handful of others followed like a gaggle of geese.

Stopping in the doorway of Doc's office, Cletus McCully held up one hand. "This is the end of the road, folks. Doc Masey can handle Crystal's wound, and something tells me Nick and Brittany could use a little time to themselves."

Although it was no secret that the good folk of Jasper Gulch liked nothing better than gossip, they did as Cletus suggested.

Doc Masey held the door while Jake, with Crystal held securely in his arms, shouldered his way into Jasper Gulch's one and only examination room. Suddenly Nick and Brittany were alone.

They both swallowed, cleared their throats, swallowed again. Brittany stared at Nick. For the life of her, she couldn't think of a single thing to say. During those brief seconds when Dawson had aimed his gun at Nick's chest, she'd thought of a dozen things she wanted to say to him if they both lived through the day. She'd wanted to tell him that she could live without his love as long as she could have the rest of him. The rest of him was standing right in front of her, yet she couldn't bring herself to make a sound.

"Are you all right?" he asked.

Her arm ached and her knees felt wobbly, but she nodded.

He took a step toward her, then stopped. "Do you have any idea how amazing you are?"

She shook her head once and managed a wavering smile. "I thought you'd left town. How did anyone know I told Dawson you were at the Crazy Horse? And how did all those people get there so fast?"

"It's hard to fathom," he said, "but I for one will never again underestimate the power of the Jasper Gulch grapevine. You did everything right. Honestly, I'm in awe. Calling Isabell 'Josie' was brilliant. You realize she's going to be even more difficult to live with from now on."

Brittany smiled at that.

"I'm afraid the fact that you really don't need me at all is going to take a little getting used to," he said.

Nick's voice was like the wind after midnight, a gentle moaning, a deep sigh, a sad, lonely sweep across her senses. He thought she didn't need him. She wanted to cry, because with him, everything came down to need and duty and responsibility.

There wasn't much she wouldn't have given up to feel his arms around her one more time. Her pride? Who needed it?

Her independence? What good was it? Her boarding house? It was a beautiful old house, but it was just a house, after all. Her marriage could have survived—it could have thrived—without any of those things. But it couldn't survive without love.

Keeping her voice as steady as possible, she looked up at Nick and said, "It looks as if you're going to get a late start back to Chicago."

Nick's blood began to do a slow boil. He and Brittany had both come close to dying today. Was she really that anxious to see him leave? He paced to the window, to the row of plastic chairs lining one wall, to the door leading to the examination room. "What is this? The old 'there's no hurry but here's your hat' routine?"

Brittany's old-fashioned dress swished around her ankles as she spun to face him. "What do you want me to do, Nick? Beg you to stay? I can't live with your guilt complex anymore. And I can't live with you and not your love. So yes, I guess there really is no hurry, but here's your hat."

She handed him the brown Stetson he'd been wearing when he'd confronted Dawson, then quietly walked into the examination room to check on Crystal.

Jake was coming out of the room as Brittany went in. He eyed his ex-sister-in-law and then his only brother. Ambling into the waiting room, he said, "You look like hell, bro."

"What did you expect?"

"You don't have to bite my head off," Jake said, strolling closer. "I'm on your side, remember? Come on. We have to give our statements, call in the Feds. You know the routine."

Nick stood slowly. "Yeah," he said, glancing at the door that led to the examination room. "I know the routine."

The brothers left the doctor's office together. Moments before a crowd of old-timers noticed them, Jake said, "I'm sorry things didn't work out between you and Brittany. I didn't think that woman would ever stop loving you."

It took everything Nick had to put one foot in front of the

other. He strode around the corner to Wyatt's office and gave his statement, then stood by while a dozen other people gave theirs. He took little pleasure in watching the Feds haul Dawson away. His mind was on Brittany and on what Jake had said about love.

He made a bee-line for the doctor's office as soon as he could, only to find the door locked tight. He tried the boarding house next. Crystal was propped on pillows on the sofa, her arm in a sling, Mertyl Gentry clucking over her like a mother hen.

"Mertyl," she said, "could I trouble you for a pot of strong tea?"

Mertyl gave Nick a calculating look. With a huff, she turned to Crystal and said, "I wasn't born yesterday, young lady. If you want some privacy, just ask."

"Then you wouldn't mind if I spoke to Nick in private?"

The old woman huffed again. "I didn't say that. I mind plenty. One pot of tea coming right up." An instant later she disappeared into the kitchen.

"Where's Brittany?" Nick asked.

Exotic green eyes met his. "She and Savannah went to the church to participate in the staged wedding."

"The wedding is still on?" Nick asked.

"You know what they say. The show must go on. Brittany was looking pretty pale when she left. She's hurting, Nick. Unless you love her, let her go."

Nick's head fell forward until his chin rested on his chest. "All I ever wanted to do was take care of her. And all I ended up doing was ruining her life. She didn't finish college because of me. There's no telling what she could have accomplished if I hadn't been so hell-bent on getting her into bed."

"Why Nicholas Colter, I never figured you for a snob."

His mouth opened, but no words would form.

"You think a college education makes one person better than the next?" Crystal winced when she tried to move her shoulder. Looking decidedly pale but determined, she said,

"Even if you added all my degrees together, I couldn't hold a candle to what Brittany has accomplished without one. She could have used the money her father left her to finish her education if that was what she wanted. And do you really believe Brittany would have slept with you if she hadn't wanted to? She loves you, you idiot. And it has nothing to do with duty or safety or guilt. I guess the only remaining question is do you love her?"

Nick dropped into a nearby chair. He'd grown up on the streets of Chicago where he'd relied on his brains and his brawn, his sense of right and wrong and his sense of duty. One by one, Crystal's words had stripped him of each and every one of those things.

How many times had he seen a hurt expression cross Brittany's face? That look had always made him uneasy, had always made him want to fix whatever was wrong. By responding with passion and desire, he'd hurt her in a hundred different ways. She loved him. She'd come right out and told him so an hour ago. The woman could do anything. And had. She'd outsmarted a criminal and was running a successful business. She was raising a child and was becoming a part of the community here in Jasper Gulch. The town was better off because of her.

Did he deserve such a woman? Probably not. Would she give him another chance? God, he hoped so.

"Where are you going?"

"To find Brittany and tell her before it's too late."

"Tell her what?" Crystal called.

The teakettle began to whistle in the kitchen just as the front door slammed. Glancing around the empty room, she muttered, "Never mind." His expression had said it all.

Chapter Eleven

The old white church was nearly full, the guests much more spirited than they were on ordinary Sunday mornings. Everyone was talking about the excitement and the events leading to Kipp Dawson's arrest. There was speculation that Wyatt McCully might run for mayor and eventually seek a higher office. Most folks were so busy talking they didn't notice the wistful expression on Louetta's face as she sat at her piano, patiently waiting.

Brittany stood in the back of church, doing her best to put on a happy face. Today's Founders' Day celebration would undoubtedly go down in history. To Brittany, it would always be the day her divorce became final.

"Do you think Nick has left town by now, Cletus?"

Cletus looked handsome in his best and only suit. His face was clean shaven, his eyes very gentle as he said, "I don't know, but folks would understand if you ain't up to doin' this."

The wedding song began, all eyes turning to the back of the church. Smoothing her hands down the skirt of her long blue dress, Brittany swallowed the lump in her throat, placed her hand on Cletus's arm, and started up the aisle. Savannah grinned from her position in the front pew with Haley, Melody and Clayt Carson.

Doing as Crystal had at practice, Brittany nodded at Forrest Wilkie as, together, they faced Reverend Jones.

A breeze came out of nowhere, fluttered Brittany's old-fashioned veil and billowing her dress around her ankles. She wasn't certain if she turned because a murmur went through the church, or if the murmur went through the church because she turned.

"It's Daddy and Uncle Jake," Savannah said with awe.

The Colter brothers stood in the doorway, the late-afternoon sun casting their features in shadow. Brittany couldn't see Nick's eyes, but she felt them on her. Removing her hand from Forrest's arm, she could only stare as Nick and Jake started up the aisle.

Nick stopped in front of her. In a voice loud enough for everyone to hear, he said, "Sorry to stop the wedding, folks, but there's something I've got to do." Glancing at the man who was acting as today's groom, he said, "Forrest, do you mind?"

The lanky rancher shook his head slowly and took several steps back.

"Nick, what are you doing here?" Brittany whispered.

"Something I should have done more than seven years ago, and every day since." Going down on one knee, he reached for her hand.

"Brittany, will you marry me? Not because you have to. Not because I'm bullying you into it."

"Nick, I—"

"Because you see, Brittany, all these years I thought I was

doing my best by you. I took all the blame, and I worked so hard to make things up to you, to make things right.''

''Nick, this isn't the place.''

''I think it's the perfect place. I want you to marry me, Brittany, because I love you.''

''What do you mean?''

''What do you mean what do I mean?''

Impatience flickered through his eyes. As one second followed another, his expression changed, and he smiled, deepening a crease on one cheek. ''Gee,'' he said. ''We sound like an old married couple already.''

Her eyelids lowered, her breath catching in her throat. And she smiled in return.

Nick wondered if she was aware of the murmur going through the church. He wondered if she was aware of the murmur going through him. There were a dozen reasons, all of them good, why she should tell him no. He squeezed her hand tighter and swallowed the knot that had formed around his voice box, praying for another answer entirely.

''Well? What do you think?''

Brittany heard the quaver in his voice, felt it in his fingertips, saw it in his eyes. In every dream she'd ever had he'd told her he loved her in the dark of night. And now, when she was fresh out of dreams, he'd proclaimed his love for her in the light of day in front of half the town.

''Uh, Brittany? Do you think you could give me an answer anytime soon? Because I'm shaking more now than I ever have in my life.''

Her first nod brought him to his feet. ''Does that mean yes?''

She nodded again. ''Yes, Nick. That means yes.''

Bringing his face within inches of hers, he said, ''I can't guarantee that life with me will ever be easy.''

She shook her head at that, because life with Nick would

most certainly never be easy. But it would be a good life, a life full of love.

Savannah was suddenly there, tugging on her father's pant leg. "Does this mean you're going to stay, Daddy?"

Nick swept the little girl into one arm. "It sure does, Savannah. I heard this town's getting a new mayor and going to be needing a new sheriff."

Keeping Brittany's hand firmly in his, Nick turned to the people all around them. "Is it all right with you folks if this wedding is real?"

A cheer went through the crowd. As Louetta started the music, Jake Colter took his place next to his brother. Forrest Wilkie started to complain that their ad was bringing more *men* to town. When Josie Callahan smiled at him before strolling across the aisle to assume her place as Brittany's matron of honor, Forrest sank into a pew, a strange expression on his face.

Reverend Jones began reading from his frayed old prayer book. Late-afternoon sunlight shone through the stained-glass windows, spilling over Gussie who cried into her handkerchief.

Brittany smiled as Nick placed the ring on her finger. Having never removed his, he simply twined his fingers around hers.

"I love you, Brittany."

Lifting her face to his, she whispered, "And I love you."

Savannah clapped. A moment later everyone else did the same.

The Jasper Gulch Founders Day celebration was a resounding success. Folks would talk about it for years to come. Along with the tale of how the brave residents of the fine community of Jasper Gulch put their heads together to capture a hardened criminal, the locals would long recall that the first annual staged 1890s wedding went down in history as the day Brittany Ann Matthews married Nicholas James Colter. Again.

Those close by heard Nick whisper, "I love you," before placing the ring on Brittany's finger.

Hours later, when the sun was gone for another day and the wind was little more than a gentle sigh in the night, he whispered those words again. And their long-awaited honeymoon began.

*   *   *   *   *

Don't you fret, there are plenty more
BACHELOR GULCH *books coming your way.*
But first, Sandra Steffen contributes to
Silhouette Romance's VIRGIN BRIDES *series.*
Watch for THE BOUNTY HUNTER'S BRIDE in July.

DIANA PALMER
ANN MAJOR
SUSAN MALLERY

In **April 1998** get ready to catch the bouquet. Join in the excitement as these bestselling authors lead us down the aisle with three heartwarming tales of love and matrimony in Big Sky country.

RETURN TO WHITEHORN

A very engaged lady is having second thoughts about her intended; a pregnant librarian is wooed by the town bad boy; a cowgirl meets up with her first love. Which Maverick will be the next one to get hitched?

Available in **April 1998.**

Silhouette's beloved **MONTANA MAVERICKS** returns in Special Edition and Harlequin Historicals starting in February 1998, with brand-new stories from your favorite authors.

Round up these great new stories at your favorite retail outlet.

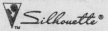

Look us up on-line at: http://www.romance.net

PSMMWEDS

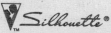

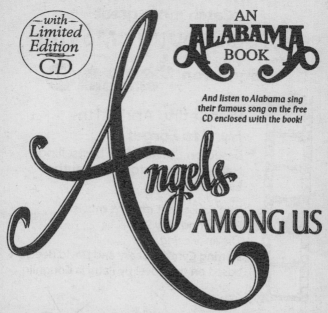
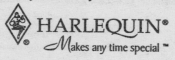

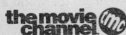

MEN at WORK

All work and no play? Not these men!

April 1998

KNIGHT SPARKS by Mary Lynn Baxter

Sexy lawman Rance Knight made a career of arresting the bad guys. Somehow, though, he thought policewoman Carly Mitchum was framed. Once they'd uncovered the truth, could Rance let Carly go...or would he make a citizen's arrest?

May 1998

HOODWINKED by Diana Palmer

CEO Jake Edwards donned coveralls and went undercover as a mechanic to find the saboteur in his company. Nothing— or no one—would distract him, not even beautiful secretary Maureen Harris. Jake had to catch the thief—*and* the woman who'd stolen his heart!

June 1998

DEFYING GRAVITY by Rachel Lee

Tim O'Shaughnessy and his business partner, Liz Pennington, had always been close—but never *this* close. As the danger of their assignment escalated, so did their passion. When the job was over, could they ever go back to business as usual?

MEN AT WORK™

Available at your favorite retail outlet!

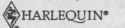 

BEVERLY BARTON

Continues the twelve-book series— 36 Hours—in April 1998 with Book Ten

NINE MONTHS

Paige Summers couldn't have been more shocked when she learned that the man with whom she had spent one passionate, stormy night was none other than her arrogant new boss! And just because he was the father of her unborn baby didn't give him the right to claim her as his wife. Especially when he wasn't offering the one thing she wanted: his heart.

For Jared and Paige and *all* the residents of Grand Springs, Colorado, the storm-induced blackout was just the beginning of 36 Hours that changed *everything!* You won't want to miss a single book.

Available at your favorite retail outlet.

Silhouette Books

is proud to announce the arrival of

A MOTHER'S GIFT

This May, for three women, the perfect Mother's Day gift is mother*hood!* With the help of a lonely child in need of a home and the love of a very special man, these three heroines are about to receive this most precious gift as they surrender their single lives for a future as a family.

Waiting for Mom
by Kathleen Eagle
Nobody's Child
by Emilie Richards
Mother's Day Baby
by Joan Elliott Pickart

Three brand-new, heartwarming stories by three of your favorite authors in one collection—it's the best Mother's Day gift the rest of us could hope for.

Available May 1998 at your favorite retail outlet.

Look us up on-line at: http://www.romance.net   PSMOMGFT